Michael Moses

FORCED EVOLUTION

An Ecological Thriller

PublishAmerica
Baltimore

© 2008 by Michael Moses.
All rights reserved. No part of this book may be reproduced, stored in a retrieval system or transmitted in any form or by any means without the prior written permission of the publishers, except by a reviewer who may quote brief passages in a review to be printed in a newspaper, magazine or journal.

First printing

All characters in this book are fictitious, and any resemblance to real persons, living or dead, is coincidental.

PublishAmerica has allowed this work to remain exactly as the author intended, verbatim, without editorial input.

ISBN: 1-60672-761-3
PUBLISHED BY PUBLISHAMERICA, LLLP
www.publishamerica.com
Baltimore

Printed in the United States of America

The planet earth is about to undergo a dramatic change that will threaten mankind's existence. Using technology and new ideals, can mankind survive this global extinction event? One man had a vision that would change the fabric of humankind. One couple's ability to adapt would have an impact on the world, and a new era of technological breakthroughs would take man to the next step in human evolution.

Dedication

I would like to acknowledge those who helped make this book a reality.
My loving wife Trish, who stood by every crazy idea I ever had and was always amazed; and my daughter, Madison, her awakening imagination has restarted mine.
My good friend Dave.
He read every draft and gave me feedback and encouragement to continue.
My motorcycle touring friends, the WILD HOGS of Nova Scotia.
Scott, Paul and Ed who read the first short draft and wanted more.

Chapter 1

Under a dim light that hardly illuminated his papers, Dr. Raymond Braemore was getting ready to deliver his findings to the United Nations. Every top-level official from every member nation is at this presentation, hoping for the magic solution to the world's problem. Most have seen their economies implode after years of sky rocketing inflation. Citizens have grown outraged, and some places, like England, are on the verge of civil war. Although most sense even war would be pointless. After all, if you are going to fight for something, it should be worth the struggle. Frankly, most countries are not worth anything during this time of crisis. Jocelyn Burris-Stone, Raymond's personal assistant, organized the slides and put the notes together in the right order. Even though her primary job was to put Raymond's thoughts in order, the outcome of the arrangement disturbed her.

His conclusions were based on fact, and agreed to by the top scientists and politicians in the world. What everyone else was going to learn today was the cost. In human and monetary terms, most countries could afford the price. And they each had to participate and make drastic choices that would unravel the moral fabric of any advanced society. Lives were at stake. Not a city, or country, but the whole planet was in crisis.

The office where Raymond and his team were preparing for the speech was wall papered with the existing political map of the world. Surrounded by names of countries, notes on the wall, big red circles where some of the land masses had disappeared, and green circles where some had appeared. A big holographic table in the middle of the room, allowed for a three dimensional view of any place in the world. Chairs were sparse. Only six chairs, the five at the holographic workstations, and the big armchair at the front of the room.

Looking at the maps from her workstation, Jocelyn thought about how none of this had been taught in her high school geography course. In 2010, things had been different; the signs were there, but no one cared enough to act on them. A few people did: Al Gore, former Vice President of the

United States, ran around the globe warning about the incoming devastation of global warming. He won awards and was extolled as someone with a vision—the vision of what could have been happening right now. He could not have foreseen the violent planetary shift that had taken place globally in the past five years. It was May 1st, 2030 AD. The world was about to end for mankind, unless Raymond's proposal was adopted that day and acted upon by the end of the summer. Raymond had no idea that he would be called upon to spearhead the radical ideas he would be presenting to the UN. He had been researching the factors that led to the creation of the United States of North America in 2020. The US could no longer use its military might to take what it wanted in the world, and to try to forcefully take Canada would have been suicide. Iraq and Afghanistan both had been expensive and pointless exercises. Troops were forced to withdraw from both countries in 2010 when the US congress recalled all of them. Too much money was spent on countries that were not going to be lap dogs for America, money that would have been better spent domestically was now going to stay in the US. Canada was a leader in the production of oil, wheat, lumber and other natural resources. There was also the technological advantage that the former country of Canada had acquired over the course of ten years from 2010 to 2020, leaving the US as a begging neighbor. The demise of the US's economy and security caused its government to hold out a carrot of unprecedented proportions: dissolve both countries and form a new one. Maintain a fair and equitable tax structure, and make sure every citizen, regardless of race, colour, religion, or economic standing is treated fairly and has a vote. This union would make the largest country in the world, and it would take the combined military of both to secure it; Canada also signed on only after agreement was made to move ahead with renewable resources, and to put the domestic welfare of all citizens first and foremost. Free enterprise in health care was abolished, and monopolies in any marketplace eliminated. Income tax was also abolished and a service tax placed on everything. Healthcare took on a public flavor, but with a twist. All services were free to citizens of the United States of North America. Drug companies were made into health care providers and could not charge a citizen for their prescribed products, lobbyists were banned; and the entire healthcare system was computerized, with information on each citizen kept within arm's reach and retrievable with a few clicks. The old United States Constitution was rewritten and some items eliminated. Firearms became illegal for the common citizen—only farmers, professional hunters, and the police were permitted to carry arms. The penalty for violating this law was severe and could result in expulsion from the country, or death. After all, if you had an illegal gun, it was presumed you were prepared to use it, and it was the legal system that came after you, seeking to protect the innocent. Anarchy had been a serious risk, but the cultural change that took place stopped it in its tracks. This change had to take place. Crime had been rampant, the cost of living approaching double digits each month and the average citizen sinking into poverty. The call to change came after a plebiscite in United States in 2021; Canada and Mexico held one in 2022. The political parties of the early 21st century lost influence and were forced to make concessions to other parties to stay in power. Most jurisdictions abandoned the federal political system all together and set up their own governing states. Ontario, Canada, led the charge with a vast manufacturing and technological base. The manufactures realized that they could not sustain the production of the past. Henry Ford may have started the revolution of every one being able to have and afford a car, but it was the autoworkers in Oshawa, Ontario who figured out that they did not have to produce thousands of cars to glut the market place. They were on board out of necessity to feed their families, but the premise was unique and kept every one employed and empowered. The days of the robot putting together cars faster than demand were over. The workers were now developing, testing and building fuel efficient hydrogen cars to order. If you wanted a car, the waiting period was four weeks, but the vehicle that arrived at your doorstep was exactly what you wanted. It even had the signatures of the craftsmen and -women who built it. These cars ran on hydrogen; ceramic motors and composites made it light, efficient and tough. It was once a radical innovation to have to wait for a car: but the cultural shift from impulse to planned purchases had taken place. Maybe it was the years of budgeting for food, or survival, that empowered the average citizen to adjust; it might have been the "enough is enough" mentality.

Every penny was precious. Every family was on the brink of losing the battle to survive, until it finally came to grips with what was happening. The generations before this one were wasteful, and caught red-handed destroying everything they thought they believed in. In 2020, after landing the first expedition on Mars and sending another group to the Moon, they started to realize that the Earth was unique for its resources. There were minerals in the inner solar system, but no oil. No air, no gases of any kind really. There was water on Mars, just below the surface, but once exposed to the atmosphere it would rapidly change to vapor. Techniques had to be discovered on how to harvest the water and convert it to a usable fuel, breathable air, and drinkable water. The now famous Garbing Reactor was what the scientists came up with. This reactor was like a heat pump that extracted energy from the atmosphere of Mars and used it to power the water extraction unit; and then the rapid change of the water to vapor was captured and powered the electrolysis that was required to break the water down to its elements, hydrogen and oxygen. The oxygen was mixed with the Martian atmosphere to create a breathable gas; the hydrogen powered the generators and the byproduct, water, was captured for drinking and irrigation. Then the byproducts of living were recycled and the process started to exponentially create an excess of hydrogen, oxygen and water. This process became the catalyst that allowed the colonization of Mars and the Moon, and the recovery and rehabilitation of Earth. It also led to the Ceramic Revolution.

The Ceramic Revolution was what the media called it. The internal combustion engine was replaced by ceramics in 2015. Retrofitting was the thing to do: retrofit the car, the lawn mower, anything that needed fossil fuels for lubrication, and power. The big manufacturers were refitting their factories to start producing ceramic based products long before it was thought that ceramics were to take over. They must have seen the logic of this; after all they made steel in ceramic containers, burned coal in ceramic furnaces—anything that required a lot of heat was usually ceramic. The materials for ceramics were plentiful, and obtaining them did not involve destroying the environment. The mining of the agents need for certain types of ceramics were permitted and regulated heavily. Underground mining with automated machines that were non-polluting and ran mostly on hydrogen became a necessity; their exhaust of water was collected and used for irrigation above the mines to grow food for the work force.

FORCED EVOLUTION

By accident, like most great discoveries, frictionless ceramics were everywhere and contributed to the release of dependence on fossil fuels. It was discovered that two common types of ceramics magnetic fields were diametrically opposed. The fields were of the exact same strength, just negative and positive. When put in very close proximity to each other, as in a piston and chamber with only microns separating them, the field gained strength and the force to have each part touch was ten times more than the force generated by the explosion of gasoline and the general forces from the standard internal combustion engine. In 2012, a complete engine was built based on the fossil fuel design. This frictionless engine required a fraction of the fuel to generate the same amount of horsepower, not to mention the lower operating temperatures of the combustion, no need for lubricants, exhaust of pure water, and total weight. It was one tenth the size of a conventional V-8, and put out more power. The revolution—the move to electrically powered vehicles, with ceramic motors and generators, and smaller batteries to store any excess—had begun. Hydrogen fuel storage was not an issue either; since less was required, the current technology for storing liquid hydrogen was already available. Filling up the tank was done once a month, either from home or from a hydrogen refill station. "Miles per gallon" was no longer in the public's vocabulary. Some items from the internal combustion days were still required. Rubber tires were still used, but again recycling regulations made sure that these were also green. It was amazing how it all tied together, but since the information age started, the world got closer, information travelled faster and new ideas and technologies could be implemented almost instantly. What used to take years of planning and retooling, was now accomplished in weeks. Computer-aided designs made it to the manufacturing floor within days. Testing the end product took about a week, and then it went into full-scale production.

The diets of the human race were also changing, as our dependency on meat was waning. The average family now consumed meat products about three times a week, compared with every meal in the early 21st century. Everything was recyclable, and this was to sustain minimal loss in resources. To say that the earth had turned green was an understatement: it was financial suicide for a company not to go green. To the praise of governments around the world, the fact that manufacturing and the business communities led the charge to environmental change took pressure off of the legislatures. They did not have to enact laws to force environmentalism, just regulations to prevent it from going too far. Farmers who had known for years that everything can be recycled were now teaching others, from the amount of grain necessary to feed livestock to the amount of methane required to run the farm: it was all precisely calculated and planned months in advance. Farms had to diversify and concentrate on all products of agriculture. Gone were the dairy farmers, beef farmers, corn farmers, just to name a few. Farmers were now able to be self-sufficient and no longer had to rely on regulations of what they could grow. Most farmers had exclusive relationships established through the government agencies with distributors. Grown locally, sold locally took on a whole new meaning and purpose as the cost to get the products to market increased.

Before the ceramic revolution, populations were moving back to cities: it was just too expensive to have two cars, big houses, and a swimming pool in the back yard. Energy consumption was out of hand and houses were being abandoned for the trek back to the city. The entire meltdown was driven by the markets: oil had spiraled out of control in 2011, reaching $1000.00 a barrel, and the economies of every country imploded. Research into bio-fuels from corn and other primary products quickly shifted to by-products: this was more successful, but not a solution to the perceived oil shortages. The market was driven by speculation: there was in fact enough oil to fuel the globe for another hundred years, but it would contribute to global warming, higher pollution, and the growing populations were not willing to let go of the excess. Something radical had to be done, and the removal of oil from the markets was the first step. Governments now controlled their resources and expropriated the big oil companies. Gone were the days of outrageous profits; a new era of regulation and production began. Fuel prices were regulated globally at $6.00 a gallon, a reduction of seventy-five percent, and set at that price for a one year term. This was the first step in the upcoming change: a global economy, a global regulatory board, and global cooperation.

Chapter 2

Raymond and his team were set to enter the UN chambers. Television coverage was global, and Raymond refused to wear makeup.

"I want to look bad, disheveled, and worried. This is not something any of us wants to contemplate, but we have to. We have to do this or die." Raymond said as he waved away the television support people. Raymond clipped on his microphone and headed to the podium. There was no applause, but everyone stood in respect of a man who was going to deliver the news no one wanted to hear. Raymond cleared his throat, adjusted his glasses and looked back at the ten-story screen to see his opening slide. Jocelyn was sitting directly in front of Raymond, papers lined out and the control of the slides was hers. They had rehearsed many times and now this was the moment.

Raymond started.

"Ladies and gentlemen, my name is Dr. Raymond Braemore. Most of you know me from my papers on the global market crisis and political change. Obviously these were enough to have you all entrust me with this project. I will not tell you anything you don't already know, but will tell you time is short and my team's findings are alarming. We thought that with all the technological and cultural changes we could avoid the global warming that has taken place: we were careful to reduce and eventually eliminate all mechanically produced green house gases; we eliminated our dependence on fossil fuels and solved the water shortage problem with a new way of doing things. Potable water is now a byproduct of living, as well as a necessity of life. Health care is no longer a crisis; we are living longer and better. But therein lies the problem. Our quality of life is too good—we live into our second century, with our zest for life undiminished. We consume less, but we still consume. When the crisis started, the ceramic revolution helped us to stop producing vast quantities of mechanically-generated Carbon Dioxide, but we overlooked the one biggest contributor—the human machine. When the crisis started some 30 years ago, the population was five billion and did not register on the measurements that were being calculated; our population is now nearly 15 billion. Human kind is the greatest contributor. So are we to stop existing? Stop procreating? No, that is not the answer.

We can still exist, and if we continue to grow the earth can still sustain another 15 to 20 billion human beings. However, the monumental shift in the climates and the earth's structure implies that it is not up to us. Our research and factual data suggests that the earth is about to revert to an earlier geological condition on a global scale, perhaps as it was before mankind descended from the trees, or even before the primordial ooze formed the first living organism. From our research stations in the Antarctic, Arctic, and equatorial bases, a significant shrinkage of the earth's diameter has been measured. Our numbers and rate of decline have all been confirmed by the measurements from the Moon and Mars. This shrinkage has accelerated from five nautical miles a year to five nautical miles a week: at this rate the earth may implode on itself within the next six months."

The congregation at the UN did all it could to conceal the horror of the news. The planet is going to destroy itself, and mankind caused its destruction. Some shouts went out from the crowd, but most remained composed and ready to hear the rest of Raymond's presentation. After a well deserved pause, Raymond continued.

"You will all be asking yourselves 'how can this be?' Consider that for over a hundred years we pumped billions of tons of carbon dioxide into the atmosphere, along with other gases and solids. When we stopped pumping the pollution, we still were breathing, the earth was still being bombarded with space dust to the tune of 10 billion tons a year. It had to go somewhere, and we had killed the earth's ability to absorb the Carbon Dioxide. Our flora was not enough to clean up the atmosphere and it just got heavier. The compression of the crust into the mantle has been on the rise for the past 10 years and just in the last year we have seen that things are getting ready to snap.

Is the earth going to implode on itself? Or burst like a big balloon? Our research suggests neither. Based on our models, what we think is going to happen is a global spin, like a child's top. This spin will last at least 24 hours, and in that time the earth's crust will, through centrifugal force, expand back to its proper diameter. If we are prepared, we can minimize the cost in human lives, but we are not going to be able to prevent casualties. Estimates are 60 percent of the population will not survive the earthquakes, tsunamis and volcanoes. We will lose any population living below one hundred feet above sea level. Anyone on the Pacific Rim or within 250 miles of a volcano will perish. Gravity is going to be reduced, possibly even eliminated, around the equator. Material is going to be expelled into space; humans may be expelled into space. The planet will always survive, and do what it has to do to maintain balance."

The audience burst into screams of horror, many realizing that their families, friends, colleagues faced imminent death: even entire countries were in danger, nations like Japan and Taiwan could be wiped out altogether. Continental plates would be torn apart and new land formed: life is about to get very tough for everyone. Raymond was prepared for questions, but they would be in vain. This was going to happen, and very soon; nothing could be done to stop it, and in some cases nothing could be done to prepare for it.

Raymond let the audience absorb the information for the next 30 minutes, and then put his hand up.

"If I could have your attention, please. Do you want to save your fellow man?"

That quieted the crowd down instantly: everyone looked at Raymond as if he was a god. There were looks of bewilderment, as if people were mentally calling out for Raymond to lead them from the apocalypse. Raymond had an answer that might save ten percent of the doomed population, maybe even twenty. He nodded to Jocelyn for the next slide.

"What you see here is a geological map of the planet earth." He pointed to the screen. "The areas of black will be gone, red will most likely be wiped out, yellow will have significant damage and loss of life, and then there's green. Green is our safety zone." The map looked like a big quilt, with the black, red and yellow lining the edges and cutting through the middle, but on both sides there were four green areas. Central Russia, Central North, South America and Australia were all considered safe zones.

"If we start to move populations now, we could evacuate many of them to safe areas. It would take three months to stockpile food, water and essentials, and to build the shelters, then another three months to move people. Everything will have to be left behind, but at least they may survive."

The delegates were starting to mutter; Raymond could see them getting anxious in their seats. He knew what they were thinking. How are we going to pay for this? What is the cost to move billions of people? Raymond put his hands up.

"Order, please," he said firmly. "Order. I know what you're thinking and that has to stop. Cost is not the issue: in fact, any monetary thinking has to cease. Our economies are based on currency, which is irrelevant in this situation. It is that easy. The cost is in human lives, not dollars and cents. We have to abandon the system now, and focus on getting the job at hand completed. For the next six months, every resource from every man, woman and child will be called upon. The survival of the human species is paramount. There can be no cost. What we have stockpiled in warehouses, grocery stores, silos, and anywhere else in the danger zones needs to be moved by all means possible. If we left the monetary system in place, people would die because they could not afford to move to the safe areas. We as a society cannot let that happen. We, as human beings, cannot allow anyone to suffer!"

This was the pinnacle of the entire speech. For the world to give up its reliance on monetary values was the revolutionary step necessary to ensure survival. Cash could no longer be king; there would no longer be a distinction between the rich and poor. Everyone will have to contribute to this effort and it is not going to be easy.

Raymond had had a lot of time to think about this. Being a Harvard graduate and very successful in his career, he was in the wealthy class. He worked hard to obtain the status symbols associated with success: it was the old American dream to be successful and rich.

The dream is now to survive.

Raymond took a long drink of water, wiped his brow and started to address the audience again.

"The amount of cash, reserves, and stocks, anything with monetary value will have to be liquidated. National debts and surpluses will no longer exist." Amid the yelling from the floor that ensued, most of the delegates were relieved. Many of the once third-world countries now had the debt relief they had been longing for; many of the developed countries no longer had the dilemma of how to spend the surplus acquired by taxes, levies and playing the stock markets.

"I know that this will mean devastation to some; in fact, the top ten percent of the population will take this very, very hard. But the reality is that if they do not accept what is happening, they will die, and their wealth means nothing." In a room filled with some two thousand of the world's leaders, there was not a sound. This information was not new; however, its implementation was, and it made sense. More details were forthcoming, but Patrick Corpert, Global Nations Secretary General, formerly the UN Secretary General, was making his way to the podium.

After all of the world's countries signed the charter of the United Nations, the name change was initiated and a new mandate was set. The Global Nations was the natural evolution of the end of the cold wars and the need for a truly global governing body. It was almost a step towards a global government, but the years of political wrangling made this impossible. Some nations were not ready to give up control, and some nations felt they were above a national policy. This was about to change in a dramatic way. With the prospect of certain countries being obliterated and others gaining millions of immigrants, a drastic new method of governance had to be implemented.

Secretary Corpert raised his hands for the delegates to quiet down, then motioned to the AV booth.

"Can you please initiate the Global Broadcasting system? This is something everyone on Earth needs to see." Digital video cameras came on and sixty seconds later, the chamber was on-line and broadcasting to every device in the world with audio, video and captions. Secretary Corpert started:

"I'm addressing the GN Council and every person on Earth. You now know of the impending disaster that will destroy vast areas of our planet, wipe out many countries, and cause the death of billions of humans and wildlife. Vast expanses of land will disappear, and the way of life that we have enjoyed since mankind started to walk upright is about to change.

I have been listening to Dr. Braemore, and consulting with the leaders of the GN Administrative body to come to the only possible resolution to this pending crisis. We all know what is at stake, and that there is no time for political posturing; the mentality of "what's in it for me" has to be put aside. There is no time to wrangle over petty details: we have to act now."

Silence fell across the chamber. After a long sip of water, Secretary Corpert continued:

"I hereby make the following motion: Be it

resolved that on this date, the first day of May in the year 2030, the Global Nations, a cooperative governing body, becomes the sole governing body of the planet earth. Also be it resolved that this governing body will be the only government on the face of the earth and all former governments will become agencies of the Global Nations. I now call for a second to this resolution."

Every hand in the chamber went up, but the President of Geneva, Guilermo Itos, was the first to yell out, "The country of Geneva seconds that resolution." Secretary Corpert nodded to the esteemed gentleman; "Thank you" was all he said. The rest of the delegates put their hands down and prepared to vote on the resolution.

"I remind you all to think of what is at stake, and to vote as a member of the human race, and not as a country looking for an advantage. If you abstain from voting, your fellow citizens will see this, and will not have a second chance. This is the one time you will have to act for all the people you represent." Looking around the chamber to make sure everyone was seated and that all the cameras were on, Secretary Corpert switched on the tally board behind him.

"It is now time to vote." The process took less than

a minute. Every delegate punched a yes or no button and the results were on the board.

To thunderous applause, the tally board showed two thousand and three votes for, and none against. Secretary Corpert waited for the applause to die down and then declared, "This resolution has passed!"

Things started to come together rather quickly after this first hurdle. The secretary was to remain in place, as it was all agreed that there would be no president. This title would not be used since it implied a hierarchy of power, and the Secretary did not want that. The cabinet, now called the working group for emergency evacuations, would work directly with Dr. Braemore to facilitate the global task at hand. The whole proceedings took less than an hour to complete and resolve; Raymond then took the podium again.

Wiping away tears after the thunderous applause and cheers, he made his way to the podium. Again his presentation flashed up on the big screen and Raymond started with part two of his speech.

"My God! I have never seen anything like it! For the first time in history, mankind is in agreement!" The members of the assembly laughed and cheered at Raymond's statement. "Now for the hard work.

How do we transition to a non-monetary society? Here are my thoughts on that."

Raymond adjusted his glasses and signaled for Jocelyn to put up the next slide. The Gaiant screen was filled with hundreds of credit and debit cards, ID cards, and passports. As the animation started to work, all the cards merged into one card that looked like a debit card with a single silver chip in the middle.

"I propose to you that the credit card companies, who have a great track record of getting cards out to almost everyone, convert their cards to a CCS, or citizen credit system. This is not to be confused with credit in terms of borrowing money, but rather credit for being a citizen. We will still require some time to adopt policies and figure out how we are going to change over to a system where the perception of money is no longer needed. This cannot be done immediately; after the disaster, if we survive, I'm sure we will accomplish this feat in record time. Until then, we have to release all debt, close all banks, and have the credit card system as it is now release any limits so that citizens can get food, fuel, and the necessary supplies to move to the safe zones." Raymond did not envy the GN Council's job of shifting the economics of mankind, but that was something to be ironed out later. "I know that convining the average citizen that they no longer have debt and money is never going to be an issue again will be easy; the people with money, power, and status are going to be the ones who will take this hard. Very hard. I can think of all the arguments, and they are going to fall on deaf ears. The world of excess has to end; the age of survival and betterment of mankind is now upon us.

So everyone will have a credit card, debit card or some way to purchase the basic needs during transition. How do we control what and how much they acquire? How do we control manufacturing? How do we control the population, and ensure that they do not throw up their hands and say they can get whatever they want when they want and as much as they want? I think this is best left for the economists who can come up with ideas for running the globe afterwards. For now, I propose a spending limit of $500.00 a day on the CCS system. If an item is required for more, they will have to call to get approval. This amount cannot be banked and resets every night at midnight GMT.

To summarize this piece of the puzzle: spending limits will be removed from all credit cards, and all prices will frozen. Vehicles can be obtained for licensed drivers for the migration, and trailers can be obtained for vehicles that can pull them. Of course these are just top level ideas: how to implement will be up to national governments." Raymond realized his thoughts were drastic, but he had to get people thinking of how to expand their ideas.

"How do we force the evolution to a non-monetary system? Implementing these ideas is a daunting task. I believe we should send the top economists from each representative region to a safe zone with in the week to start developing the procedures and policies we need to follow once mankind is ready to resume day-to-day life." Raymond could see that it was time for a break; his audience was getting overwhelmed with details and digesting the information they had just received. "I would like to take an hour's break. I know that planning that has to start immediately and people have to start getting the logistics in motion. When we reconvene, I will have binders on your desks outlining the steps necessary in the next few weeks to start moving the populations to the safe zones, what resources need to go first and what needs to be done. We will meet back here in one hour." The crowd dispersed as Raymond and his team left the stage and headed back to their office.

Jocelyn asked Raymond, "Dr. Braemore, do you think that this plan will succeed? There are so many questions—how will we implement these changes and deal with the current class structure and security?"

Raymond held his finger to his lips. "Please, let's just concentrate on the task at hand. It isn't up to us to figure out how to implement something that may not matter if we do not survive." The team walked silently down the hallway. Once in the office, no one spoke; Raymond was left with his thoughts and papers while everyone else munched snacks from the trays of food.

When the hour expired, everyone was back in their seats and waiting for Raymond. His team was in place, but Raymond had not yet taken the stage. He was in a side conference with the Secretary of the GN, the President of the United America, the Prime Minister of the European Union, and the President of the Asian States. The discussion was centered on the safe zones and how to utilize resources and space available. Raymond was explaining that high-rise buildings had to be abandoned, and the rural areas of existing cities would be the best places for refugee camps. This was based on sheer numbers and the percentages of survival during a natural disaster. Earthquakes and tsunamis were the main concern; secondary was the amount of volcanic ash that was going to be sent into the atmosphere, diminishing the amount of sunlight. Past research into these disasters almost guaranteed that for the next two years after the shift, nothing would grow, and temperatures were going to be very, very cold.

All five men shook hands and Raymond made his way back to the stage. Removing his glasses, Raymond started the second half of his speech.

"Ok," he said, "the next part of this plan is start to mobilizing the armed forces and engineers towards the safety zones. We will need to build housing, shelters, distribution warehouses and an infrastructure to support billions. I have been assured by the leaders of these areas that military forces and a civilian workforce have been granted unrestricted travel. Workers from manufacturing factories will be included in the civilian work force and residents in the safe zones will become support personnel for them. Based upon census data, United America will prepare to receive nine hundred and fifty million people in the central area of the North American continent, particularly in Alberta, Utah, Missouri, and Manitoba. The Asian

States will house three billion in the areas of Kazakhstan, Mongolia and Russia. The European Union will host three billion in the Niger, Chad and Sudan. Australia and the surrounding regions of New Zealand, Indonesia, and New Guinea will move to the central part of Australia near Alice Springs in the Northern Territory, an estimated population of one billion. And the final safe zone to house two billion is Brazil, Bolivia and Paraguay. You will find the maps outlined in your binders.

In the next two months construction will have been well underway for shelters and infrastructure, every available person will have to work on these projects, and migrations will have started. As people arrive, they will be given tasks to complete and assist with the construction.

I know one question you have been asking is about materials and resources. This is a global disaster, and we are fighting to ensure the survival of mankind. In previous extinction events, almost everything perished, so using the resources at hand is a must. A good example is if you have to clear cut a forest, and then do it. Forests will grow back, and chances are high that it would be destroyed anyway. Let's ensure the survival of all species, flora and fauna. I do not think the oceans will be as fortunate, and many species will perish.

We need to stockpile everything we can think of to ensure survival for at least two years, maybe three, since models predict that we will not have enough sunlight to grow food for a long time."

Raymond had gone through all of his slides; he now began the finale of his ground-breaking speech.

"In closing I'm sure a lot of you are thinking how can this be accomplished. Simply put, we have to do it; we have to ensure our survival as a species. Everyone will have to work together; we cannot allow our society to collapse into anarchy. We have overcome so many obstacles to get to where we are today: now we have one more. If we all work together mankind can truly shape the outcome of the greatest natural disaster to ever strike our planet." The thunderous applause was followed by cheers and calls for Raymond to lead the teams. Secretary Corpert immediately asked for a vote on the nomination of Dr. Raymond Braemore to be the Director of the Global Survival Initiative. Again the vote was unanimous, and Dr. Braemore graciously accepted the position with the understanding from all the delegates that he had the power to do whatever it would take to get this job done. Again, there was no dissention: he had one hundred percent support.

Chapter 3

Richard and Maryann Steves lived in a small community just outside of White River Junction on the Vermont-New Hampshire border. When they both retired from the 9-to-5 rat race, their lifestyle became one of passion for creating things that would not have an overall environmental cost, and be healthy for their consumers, so they set up their modest farm to supply the local farmers market with produce, dairy and other grocery products. Richard, a former engineer with the New Hampshire Power Authority, had extensive expertise in solar and wind power generation, which he put into practice for his operation. He took pride in the fact that he was "off" the grid and could supply all his power needs with the technology of the day. His windmill generated a near-constant supply of power and the solar array provided power storage for the barns and his home. Maryann was an expert cook, and spent much of her time making preserves and breads for the farmers market.

The phone rang, and Richard checked the call display. It was his sister calling from Maine.

"Hi, Sis. How are things along the coast?"

She was frantic. "Oh my God, do you believe what is happening? Mom and Dad are terrified, the kids are in a state of shock and I don't know what to do!"

Samantha, youngest of Richard's siblings, lived in Bar Harbor, Maine: her house sat on the coast with a couple of acres of beach frontage. When her husband was lost at sea ten years ago, their parents moved in and helped with the raising of her four children. The kids were in their teens, but still very reliant on their mother.

"We don't know what to do! The government says we should evacuate to Utah, but I don't want to leave. This is my home, and you know mom and dad are too old to travel, they couldn't handle the trip. Richard, I'm scared."

Richard could tell by the tone of her voice that she was ready to lose it. The strain was becoming too much. "Sam, what's been going on there?"

"We've had a few storms that were very violent." She paused; when she resumed, her voice began to waver almost uncontrollably. "And each storm was so powerful that the ground would shake. There are shingles all over the yard, I think they are ours. Dad suggested I get some plywood for the windows, I'm going to have to try to get into town and see if I can find some."

Richard could tell this was something that Samantha could not comprehend and she was really calling to ask for help. Most of the Steves family was too stubborn to ask for help, but they were not too proud to accept it when it was necessary. Richard knew that this was her way of reaching out.

"Sam," Richard said in a very calm voice, "do you need help? Maryann and I can be there in a week, once we get the farm closed up."

"Oh God, would you come?" Samantha started to cry.

"There now, Sam, of course we'll come, we're family and you need help. I have a lot of work to do around here first, but as soon as I get it finished we'll be there—I would say early next week."

Sobbing and barely to get any words out Samantha said very softly, "Thank you, we love you guys."

"I know. Here's what I need you to do. Get a pen and paper, I'll give you a shopping list."

"Ok, I have that right here, what do you want me to get?"

"You'll need sheets of three quarter inch plywood, enough for all the windows and one sheet for each door. Get fifty pounds of three-inch nails, ten rolls of one-eighth inch poly house wrap, two staple guns and ten boxes of ½" staples."

Richard also wrote down his list, and checked it to make sure that he did not miss anything.

"That should do it for now; we'll pick up anything we need once we get there."

"Ok. Please hurry—I'll tell everyone we can expect you next week."

"Yes, early next week. I'll have Maryann bring some supplies as well. Sam, don't worry, we'll be there."

"I know, Richard, I know. Thank you."

"You're welcome, Sam. See you soon." Richard hung up the phone.

"Maryann, we've got to make a trip," Richard said, as he grabbed a notebook and headed towards the kitchen. He sat down and started to plan things out in his head.

Maryann started to object: from the radio reports of mass evacuations from the coasts, this did not make sense. She knew of the mass migrations away from imminent danger; but she also knew that the government could not force families to evacuate from the place they felt the safest—their homes. She would stand by her husband no matter what, and she knew this routine. Every time Richard had a project or plan, he would sit down at the big oak dining table in the kitchen and get very quiet. This was her cue to put the twelve-cup coffee pot on and defrost some tea biscuits. She also knew to grab a note pad and pen: Richard was overly thorough, but had a tendency to get so caught up in his plans that he only wrote down about half of his thoughts. Maryann caught the rest.

When the coffee was ready, Richard accepted his mug from Maryann and they got to work. "Thanks hon," was all he said. He licked the tip of the pencil and started to write a list, while talking aloud.

"We'll need to pack as much as we can carry, and take the trailer."

Maryann interrupted, tears forming in her eyes. "We're not coming back, are we Richard?"

That question brought home the reality that they were evacuating their home, and the stark realization that they will never be back.

"No, hon. We won't make it back."

"Then we should make our home ready for

someone else. I mean if there are survivors, they will need a place to live, and you know that our house will survive. You built it to last through almost anything, power, storage, even the animals and farmland—you even called it our little self-sufficient block of paradise."

"You're right; someone could find this place one day and take up stakes right here. They can use the generators, tractor and keep up the farming operation we have built."

Maryann was nodding and writing. "They can use the food we have stored to survive for at least a couple of years until things get back to normal and the farm is producing again."

"Right. I'll make sure that whoever finds this place will have no problem setting up the systems. We'll have to make a video and leave notes, but we can do this."

Maryann was the first to move into action. She immediately opened the pantry to take an inventory. She would have to determine what they needed to take and what could be left behind. Richard grabbed his video camera and went to the generator building. He began taping and explaining each system: the windmill, the solar array, the batteries, and the water system. From there he walked through each barn, introducing the animals by name. He then turned his attention to the machinery, going over his electric tractor at some length. He walked around the property, talking all the time about where to plant crops, when to harvest grain for the animals, and how to make flour. He walked into the woods where a fast-flowing stream provided crystal clear water to the homestead. He explained the history of the stream, and the system they used to recover the water. When he was finished with the water, he stopped; six hours had passed and the light was starting to fade.

Walking back into the house, he was arrested by Maryann's voice yelling "Take off those shoes!" He looked up to find her smiling as she scolded him.

"Yes ma'am." Richard complied. This was a regular occurrence, since he usually got so caught up in his projects that when he came into the house, he was in a fog of heavy thought, still running over the job in his mind. "With your permission Gov'nor, may I enter the abode?"

"Of course, but if I have to tell you about your footwear again, I'll have you beheaded!"

Richard was laughing as he sat down at the table. He started to make his list of things to do. *The power* system can be dismantled in the morning, batteries will last for at least three days, and the solar array will have to be stored. Then the barn and the animals...his expression turned to puzzlement.

"I hope the animals will survive."

Maryann looked up from her inventory list. "I'm not sure. We can't just leave them in the barn, they would die of starvation."

"Yes...but since we let them graze, I think I'll leave the back doors open to give them some shelter and let them run loose on the property. I think our fences will keep most of them here. The chickens we can slaughter and take with us." Richard wrote that down on his list; Maryann added coolers to hers.

Over the next three days Richard and Maryann worked feverishly to get everything accomplished. On the eve of their departure to Maine, they had one last coffee on their porch.

"I'm going to miss this place," Richard said in a somber tone.

"Me too. But, I'm sure someone will make a nice home out of it again, and appreciate all the hard work we did to ensure they could survive." Maryann took one last sip of coffee and snuggled up to Richard; they watched the sunset over the mountains and didn't say a word. Both knew this would be the last time they watched the sunset from their home.

In the morning, Richard checked everything one last time and was satisfied with the work. "Perfect, the way it should be. Now, we should leave a note. Mrs. Steves, can you take a letter?"

Giggling, Maryann sat down and produced a new piece of parchment paper and a waterproof pen. "Ready, sir; please start."

Richard up stood straight and put his hands on imaginary lapels, cleared his throat and started with "If our home has survived…"

When the note was finished, Richard kissed Maryann and gave her a big hug. "I'll put this on the door, and then we can head off to Maine. Meet you in the truck."

Richard taped the note to the inside glass of the door, turned to look around at their home one more time and then closed the main door. Then he closed and secured the screen door, and put the key under the porch. He walked slowly to the car, a small tear falling down his cheek. He got into the truck, pushed the start button and put it in gear. As they made their way down the driveway, they didn't speak: Maryann looked back at her home, barely able to focus through her tears, while Richard stared straight ahead, watching the road and focusing his thoughts on his family in Maine.

***

Three months have passed, and the biggest mobilization in mankind's history is taking place. Cruise ships have been circling the globe, evacuating people from islands. Massive fleets of trucks, trains, and aircraft have been moving products to the central zones. Refugee camps are expanding and the military has been put in place to police the camps. Raymond watched the progress via satellite and GPS communications, and liked what he saw. The entire population of earth has come together with a colony mentality to build and prepare. One of the unforeseen benefits was the security of each zone: since there were no money worries, resources were shared, borders were nonexistent any more, and there was little to fight over. Property crime was non-existent; when the monetary system was abolished, people developed a better respect for others' belongings. If there was something they saw and wanted, they went and got it. Social crimes were still committed, but that could be attributed to stress; that too had declined by eighty percent per capita from previous years.

Religious freedoms were just that, freedoms. The Muslim and Christian religions gave up their battle for whose God was better: now they are both concentrating on helping their fellow man to survive. Some cultural differences caused tensions, but were quickly overcome due to the understanding that everyone was in this together. What strange bedfellows disasters make, Raymond thought. There is no way that this could happen in better times. No politician would give up his power or status; no banker would lose vast fortunes without a fight. The chance that three months from now, the earth could implode and wipe out everything has forced great changes.

The main drop off point for evacuees on the Eastern seaboard of North America was New York City: its rail and vehicular infrastructure and facilities to handle twenty or more cruise ships at once made it a logical choice. Steve Bowing of Hamilton, Bermuda, was one such evacuee. He had never been off the island, yet worked nearly every day of his life to survive. The hope of survival was the only thing that made him realize he had to abandon his home; his family and friends would not leave, since they all thought it was hopeless. There won't be any survivors, they told him; no one can live through what is going to happen. Steve disagreed, and pleaded with others to join him. No one took him up on the offer. As Steve arrived in New York, the majesty of the skyline took his breath away; everything was so clear, so quiet. He did not know that New York had been evacuated months ago—the only traffic was buses, trucks and trains moving people to the middle of North America. Airlines were no longer flying, and the daily commuters were long gone. New York City was a ghost town. The routes out of the city was lined with military and police officials who volunteered to stay behind to ensure a smooth flow of traffic, and a small army from the Red Cross gathered supplies for the masses in evacuation zone one. Security for the Red Cross was the former Navy SEALS, who had orders to disable any attempts to disrupt the supply mission. Even though they knew the use of deadly force was authorized, they were trained to avoid this at all costs. People are panicked, and most who tried to interrupt the mission were uninformed. Officers would explain first, assist in relocating, and as a last resort use deadly force. Most of the people who were confronted did not know, and soon joined in helping the Red Cross, until they could get out of the city.

    Jenna Vierra was one such person. She had

fallen on hard times in the last three years: she lost her job, lost a very costly divorce and had eventually been left homeless. She was a former stock broker, university educated, and once lived the good life in a Manhattan apartment. Her knowledge of what was happening in the world was nonexistent. She couldn't figure out why everyone was leaving; when she tried to get an answer, she was brushed off as a crazy homeless person. She had been lost in the fog of despair for the past two months, and being on the verge of panic made matters worse. It wasn't until a scouting team found her asleep in a Key grocery store that she finally got the answers she needed: they were terrifying answers, but they lifted the fog she had been living under and snapped her out of the curse that had kept her from being a productive human being. She wanted to help, needed to contribute and get away from New York City. The team took her to the main base in Manhattan, and then on to the transfer station where she met Steve. Both were waiting to board the train and were in complete awe of the precision and organization of moving thousands of people. Crowds were foreign to both, and they gravitated towards each other.

    Formal introductions were made when Jenna stepped on Steve Bowing's toes.

"Goddamn it, woman, watch me toes!" Jenna turned around; Steve smiled and said "Please?" They both laughed and Jenna smiled back.

"I'm Jenna Vierra, and I'm so sorry for stepping on your toes. Very sorry."

"No problem. I had my steel-toed sandals on," he chuckled. "I'm Stephen Bowing, but everyone calls me Steve and I should be the one apologizing, I'm not familiar with this area and wasn't paying attention. I have never seen so many people wandering around in utter shock."

"I know, it's like all the light bulbs have been turned off."

Steve got the joke right away. "And everyone is still home." They both laughed at the same time, and Jenna started to feel very shy, looking away and down at the ground. "So Jenna, where is the rest of your family?"

This caused her to look up at Steve, she saw the concern in his eyes. "I don't have any family any more. It hasn't been a very good year, and I think I only have one new friend now."

Steve nodded. "Yes, I would say you have a new friend now."

Both knew right away they should stick together: they could sense each other's survival instincts, and loneliness. Steve and Jenna got on the train for the three-day journey into the unknown. They were among the last to be evacuated from New York.

The train journey was uneventful. Everywhere along the tracks was abandonment: cars, houses, even livestock left to fend for themselves. People took what they could and left all the creature comforts behind. Overgrown lawns had become fields of long grass. Everything was a deep green: pollution was no longer spewing from factories that had shut down months ago. Farming had ceased and everything looked untouched, except for the machinery, and the animals. Some fields were full of rotting carcasses of domesticated animals that had been neglected; the skies were full of buzzards and crows, picking away at the leftovers. The entire human population had simply packed up and left for the safety zones. Vehicles were not permitted, only authorized methods of transportation, trains, buses, and tractor trailers with supplies were allowed into the zones. Cars were abandoned at the border markers, and any that remained on the highways had been plowed off to the side by the military. Steve and Jenna stared out of the window of the train as it entered Salt Lake City. A city of one million had exploded into a city of 20 million.

Shelters were constructed as far as the eye could see; each family was allotted two bedrooms, a kitchen and a bathroom. Supply stores were spread out every 10 blocks, and identity cards were used as a method of tracking how many supplies each family received. Even though currency was no longer needed, rations were in place to ensure everyone got a fair share. The length of time everyone would be spending here was not known; supplies were stock piled for a two-year stay, but would that be enough? No one knew, or could predict. When the adjustment came, it was not known if any one would survive at all, but that was a chance they had to take.

Ray followed the progress in the four safe zones, and was impressed with the speed and efficiency with which materials and people were moving. He thought how good the world had become at mobilizing for wars, while being so very bad at helping our fellow man. It was good to see things coming together.

Ray turned to Jocelyn. "You know, if there wasn't a global crisis right now, I think we could accomplish great things. How everyone pulled together, put their differences aside and built four great cities in less than six months is amazing. Take money and religion out of the picture and mankind can do anything."

Jocelyn agreed. "You know, Ray, you're the one that pulled this all together. With your leadership and knowledge, leaders of other countries acted fast to approve your plan and put it in motion. Without your vision and sanity, we would all be savages, tearing at each other's throats to gather as much meaningless crap as we could find in hopes of taking it with us. The entire Eastern seaboard would be oblivious of the pending disaster and millions if not billions of people would perish. I know you're too modest to accept the praise, but it's true, every human on the face of this planet owes you their lives. In fact, when it is all over, every person will remember you as we start to rebuild, the reasoning behind the growth we have all experienced, the dedication to the survival of mankind and the abandonment of the monetary-based society that was destroying the planet."

The evacuations were almost complete: over one hundred million people had gathered in the Utah zone over the past six months and the food supplies were holding well. Logistically, all roads lead to Utah, with communities sprouting up all over the country side. In Russia, China and Brazil, it was the same, an orderly gathering of nearly 30 percent of the world's population. The shock of losing everything had given way to the great gains mankind stood to reap. No more dependence on money, class structures, or the routines that put the world in jeopardy.

The communities in China led to one of the heaviest pollution zones in the world, and the Chinese only wanted what the West had for decades. Factories spewed out carbon at astronomical rates; construction was non-stop, with around-the-clock building. Materials were being consumed at a pace never before seen, and would never be seen again—that is, using old traditional methods. New, renewable methods of construction were now being planned for and worked on. The new towns and cities that were being constructed consisted of renewable materials, and carbon fibers had replaced steel for strength, and concrete was recycled from other buildings.

The reintegration of concrete was one of the biggest breakthroughs of the century. Old concrete was crushed and reanimated with organic byproducts that enabled it to once again be used as a fresh and stronger material for building. The R factor for insulation increased, the need for a rebar was eliminated, and now a newly-constructed building of concrete was more energy efficient, stronger and recyclable. Given a lifetime of over a hundred years, these structures would last many generations and provide a strong and safe environment to live in.

Everything was recycled, nearly eliminating the need for new raw materials. The raw materials that were required were highly regulated; it usually took longer to obtain a permit to get the materials than it did to recycle something to take its place. The re-useable revolution gathered steam from every vantage point. It soon became part of construction culture to invent new ways to obtain materials required through waste products or recycled buildings. Energy was not wasted on refining, but used in recycling.

Raymond sometimes could not believe how it all came to be. Here were warring countries, religious factions, and economic Giants, now working side by side for the preservation of mankind. Not only theirs, but everyone else's well being was being considered. Raymond figured that very soon, survival would be first and foremost. The earth was not going to let the centuries of neglect go unnoticed. When it was time to establish a new equilibrium, the ride was going to be violent, rough and deadly.

Earthquakes in the magnitude of 9 to 11 on the Richter scale would strike: some buildings would be severely damaged, others would be flattened altogether. Landmarks like the Washington Monument, the Eiffel Tower, the CN Tower, the Taj Mahal and the Burj Al Arab Hotel will succumb to the devastation. The Western States, the Eastern Seaboard, Western Europe, Australia, New Zealand, Japan and Antarctica will all be under water. There is no way to know whether sea life will survive; it is only known for certain that many species will perish, and the tsunamis will wipe out forests and farm lands.

Of the entire relocated population, scientists predict that at least 50 percent will not survive the quakes, and it will be up to the remaining people to start to rebuild. Computer models predict that the shaking will last for eight to ten days, the water will continue on for another two weeks; after that equilibrium will slowly be reestablished, and mankind can venture out and start to rebuild.

The knowledge that the old ways caused this catastrophe would have to be used to the best advantage possible, in addition to the new ways that helped populate Mars and put a base on the moon. Ways that enabled the dependence on fossil fuels to diminish, and renewable energies to be used. Preserving our new way of life for generations to come has become the normal way of doing things; we are going to better ourselves, our understanding of who we are, of how lucky we are, and how we can improve our way of life without destroying our environment.

As Raymond turned to look out the window of the command and control centre, he noticed something unusual about the sky. It was noon in Utah, and the sun was high in the sky, yet it had the reddish glow of a late summer sunset. Since the evacuation of most of the weather and environmental monitoring sites along the coasts had been completed, only the United States Geological Society's new monitoring station in Utah provided all the meteorological data for the Utah Zone. Just as Raymond thought he should call the USGS to get an update, his phone rang.

"Dr. Braemore."

"Raymond, it's Stuart at the USGS."

Stuart Matheson was the lead geologist, and a new friend of Raymond's. They became acquainted when Raymond was researching what was going on with the global situation. Stuart and Raymond spent countless hours reviewing data taken from satellite measurements and surveys to come up with the hypothesis of the earth's shrinking, then they looked at the geological data to determine that there was going to be a rebound effect. It was this discovery and subsequent testing that predicted exactly what was about to happen.

"Hi, Stuart," Ray said. "I bet you're calling to let me know things have started."

"Yes, there is some violent activity along the Pacific rim, and Greenland. The active and dormant volcanoes have started to erupt. At last count there were 600 eruptions around the globe. Material is now flowing into the atmosphere at roughly five hundred metric tons a minute." His voice did not sound calm, the tonal quality slightly elevated. "But there's something more disturbing, Raymond."

Raymond had a second to think—what could be more disturbing than all the volcanoes on earth erupting at once?

Stuart's voice became rough; Ray could tell panic was setting in. "Ray, Yellowstone is sinking, and it may explode."

"What do you mean, sinking, Stuart?"

"I mean the entire park is sinking. Thirty meters so far, and it could get a lot worse."

Raymond knew Yellowstone was only about 200 miles from Salt Lake City, and any event there could be catastrophic for the Evacuation Command Center.

"Tell me what you know." Raymond's voice very cool and calm.

"Yellowstone has always been a geological hot spot having been the scene of a super volcano about 650,000 years ago. It's a weak spot in the earth's crust, and it looks like this super volcano is waking up. If it erupts, most of Wyoming will be covered with ash and millions of tons of debris will be thrown into the atmosphere in one big bang. Ray, you have to stop the evacuations and recall your people, then move any evacuees out of Wyoming if you can." This was the first time anyone had called him Ray.

"What's the status Stuart? What are the birds showing us?"

"From the GEOS two and six, covering the Eastern Seaboard and Greenland, it looks like the ice shield is vaporizing off of Greenland: this will raise the ocean level by nine percent, and from GEOS twelve the East Antarctica Ice Sheet has started to melt and break up. It looks like if these two go then the sea levels will rise by fifty to sixty meters in the next two weeks. New volcanic activity can be seen in Antarctica, with twelve new volcanoes and hundreds of vents. Yellowstone has dropped 30 metres in a radius of about 100 miles to the North." Stuart was very professional: his data had to be accurate or it wouldn't be released. His reputation was put on every word out of his office. Raymond knew this all too well, and it didn't sound good.

"Sixty metres! What's going to be covered?"

"Hang on a second; I've got more data coming in now." There was a pause, Raymond could hear the activity on the other end of the phone, people yelling like it was a sporting event: cities were gone, and tsunami warnings were going out, but to no avail. The populations of those cities had been evacuated for weeks—at least he hoped so. He knew not everyone would evacuate, but he also knew that the crews were told to leave those who did not cooperate behind. That was perhaps his toughest call, since he knew they would all be dead when the earth started to equalize.

"Ray, I have some more data coming in. We have all the birds online now, and it does not look good."

Raymond interrupted. "Have a detailed report ready within the hour. I'm going to call the Global Community leaders together in the situation theater: we all need to know what is going on, and what to expect. And Stuart, do not include Yellowstone in your presentation—I don't think that this is something anyone needs to know about at the present moment. I'm prepared to accept total responsibility for this decision."

"Ok," said Stuart. "do you want sat links too?"

"That's a great idea. Hang in there; I'll talk to you again at, say, 14:30 hours?"

"Done. And Ray?"

"Yes?"

"Thanks for saving my family."

Raymond pressed end on the phone. He knew he hadn't saved Stuart's family; he just helped facilitate the exchange of information. Stuart and his team had saved themselves, and millions of humans around the world, but as scientists he imagined that they did not see it that way.

Raymond walked out on to the C&C floor. General Ortez was in command when Raymond summoned him over.

"General, we need to move to code red. Stop the evacuations and recall all personnel."

"What's happening, Dr. Braemore?"

"Mother Nature has started to clean house." With that, General Ortez picked up the intercom phone.

"General Ortez here. Code Red. Recall everything, stop evacuations and get our people back to the safe zones."

Raymond walked slowly to his office; he just gave the order to let billions of people die, and the weight on his shoulders just increased. He weighed the options and decided not to call for an evacuation of Wyoming. The resources were not there. He had known there would be losses; but he had not expected them this close to a safe zone. He slammed his door and called Jocelyn.

"It's me," he said in a very low tone. "Call an emergency meeting for 14:30 hours. We need to present a brief on what's happening." He hit the end button, threw his phone to the desk and looked out the window. No emotion was showing on his face, yet from the corner of his left eye a tear flowed down his cheek.

At 14:30 precisely, the gathered assemblies in Utah, Moscow, Xi'an, Palmas, and Nairobi were brought up on the video screens. A 360° view of each assembly could be broadcast, with two screens in the middle of each assembly for the presenter and their data. Raymond took the podium and banged his gavel.

"I would like to call this meeting to order.

Welcome, everyone, and I'm glad to see that you have made it to the safety zones. Current numbers indicate that we have two billion people accounted for, and with the recall of troops and evacuation personnel another addition two hundred million should be safe by this time next week.

Before I turn this briefing over to Stuart Matheson of the United Geological Society, I want to stress that no one is to be denied access to the safe zones. If people can find their way without our assistance they are to be registered and welcomed the same as the evacuees. We are not in the business of counting heads and settling for numbers: this is mankind we are saving. Our lives we are preserving." There was no outward opposition to the statement; most of the faces on the video screens were pale and blank. What everyone had been warned about was happening, and disbelief seems to have taken over.

"I now turn you over to Stuart Matheson." Stuart's face appeared on the center video screen, albeit rather large. His nervousness was apparent.

"Thanks, Ray—um, Dr. Braemore. Members of the assembly, please direct your attention to the video screen. We are going to uplink the GEOS satellite system, the Terra mapping system and the

CRAY supercomputer's scenario building system to show you what is happening right now, and a timeline of the next 24 through 72 hours. Then we will move a week, and a month ahead. Our estimation of the devastation is based on sea levels, Richter scale measurements and tsunami wave heights.

"From the current GEOS system, you will see that the glacial ice has begun to melt at an extremely accelerated rate on Greenland and the East Antarctic Ice Shelf. This makes up roughly 87 percent of the ice on the planet. As this ice melts, coastal water levels will rise by about 60 meters. This compounded by the volcanic activity along the Pacific rim, Antarctica and Greenland, and earthquakes along the Canadian Shelf, Brazilian Coast, and the Mediterranean, will cause tsunamis to deliver the water at an accelerated rate."

The next slide that Stuart put up drew screams and howls from what seemed to be the entire population of the world. It was unbelievable what people saw. In a time lapse of only seventy two hours, thirty percent of the world's land mass disappeared. Europe and the British Isles were wiped out in two hours; the North American and South American continents were no longer joined, because Central America, Cuba and the Carribbean islands, and most of Mexico, were wiped right off the map. Florida disappeared. African and European countries along the Mediterranean countries were gone, as were Japan and Indonesia. Papua New Guinea was turned into a very small island and Australia shrank by about 30 percent. New Zealand remained and Antarctica developed into a new land mass of various volcanic islands, very active and pouring magma freely into the ocean.

"From this three-day animation, you can see it looks bad. But, but," Stuart stumbled, "the next wave of activity will be even worse for the remaining and new coastlines." Up came a slide of the newly-formed land masses: this time line was 96 to 120 hours out. "Since most of the coastlines are now uniform, and as there is no land between continents the pebble affect will erode them further. What I mean by this is if you throw a pebble in a lake the waves radiate out from the point of origin, strike the shore, or something solid and bounce off that object and head back to the point of origin. This will take place with tsunamis that will travel at 500 to 1000 kilometers per hour: the time it takes for the energy to be dissipated will last at least four days. Each time one of these strikes a shoreline, it will wipe the shoreline clean."

He paused to wipe his brow, and even though he could only see a very small picture in picture of each assembly, he knew the news was not being taken well.

"Finally, after 168 hours or one week, we should have the main event. It is our best estimate that the earth will correct the imbalance over the span of 24 hours; it will expand by ten percent, and then shrink by five percent. Volcanic activity and earthquakes during this time will be felt all over the globe at a factor 6 to 7 in the safe zones, and 9 to 10 along the coasts." Stuart paused. He wanted everyone to absorb this information. There was more bad news to come, but this time not from him. Raymond returned to the podium.

"Good job, Stuart. Thank you." Ray removed his glasses. "I would now like to bring your attention to Dr. Rachel Grossman, former director of the NOAA and now head of the research department of Global Meteorology here in Utah."

"Thank you, Dr. Braemore. What we have studied and ascertained from models and previous scientific data from other planets like Jupiter is that the atmosphere will also correct itself, much in the same way the planet is doing. The atmosphere is a balloon surrounding another balloon, that being earth. As the planet flexes and changes shape, so does the atmosphere, and it is this change in shape that will cause it to cleanse itself." Dr. Grossman's slide was very simple: it showed the earth with the new configuration of continents, and what appeared to be a dirty brown hurricane sitting over the Atlantic, spewing its contents into outer space. "As the oceans' currents shift, the engines that drive the trade winds and the weather patterns will cease, except for one gigantic storm system that will form in the middle of the Atlantic ocean. Since the trade winds and currents will have stopped due to the influx of new fresh water into the system and a balancing of the globe itself, this storm will be stationary for three to four days. During that time, the vortex that forms will rotate counter-clockwise and reach heights of 400 to 500 kilometers, high enough to touch the vacuum of outer space, which will drive this storm system even more." She switched slides, and a familiar image appeared.

Most people recognized the animation of what happened when the earth was struck by a huge comet, the plumes of ash entering space and then covering the planet with debris, causing the last ice age. However, this slide was a little different.

"I know you have all seen this animation before, but please take notice of the material being expelled. This material will be water, carbon, ash, and atmospheric gases; nothing to cover the earth and block the sun's rays. In fact, we anticipate that this material will either congeal as another moon or possibly make its way to the moon's gravitational field and become a satellite there." Dr. Grossman paused for a few seconds to get a drink of water and deliver her final remarks.

"Finally, the last slide should give us an indication of wind speeds and affects of the massive super storm we have called "Gaia". This storm, while creating a balance in the atmosphere, will also act as the engine to jump start the trade winds and the global climate. During the storm, winds may reach 100 to 150 kilometers per hour across the entire planet. We anticipate that these winds will only last two to three hours. During this time Gaia will generate the forces necessary to jump start the ocean currents, mix the fresh water with the salt and start the process. We anticipate that the shift in the earth's axis will increase rotational speed and the length of time from sunrise to sunset will be 11 hours, therefore our days will be 22 hours long instead of the 23.93 hours. There will be a lot of adjustments, but it is our opinion that after this is all over, and the atmosphere is restored with the proper ozone, and atmospheric gases, we will all welcome the changes. It's going to be a rough ride, but Gaia will dissipate in a matter of hours once the balance is established. Our weather patterns after Gaia is gone will start out mostly clear, with no storms or precipitation for a month; then evening rain showers will start to appear along the terminator line, about 200 kilometers on each side. This trend will continue until the atmosphere reaches the proper humidity level and starts to produce weather during daylight hours."

Dr. Braemore again took the podium.

"I would like to thank Dr. Grossman for her insight and good news at the end of a devastating event. I think we are all in agreement that what we are witnessing is a correction on a global scale. There is nothing more we can do, except hold on and hope to survive."

"I want to call your attention to the middle display. It is the Command and Control Center in Utah. This is our base of operations, and we will keep this video on the air until the disaster has passed. I ask that you keep the evacuees informed of everything that is going on: we have also published these presentations and video on the Global Network."

Raymond then looked straight into the cameras, stern and in control. "We are about to see what Mother Nature can do. We are about to see the wondrous spectacle of maintaining a balance on a global scale. Even though we are observing the ecosystem in action, I pray that we all survive to become part of this system. Take care, and be safe. I will see you all again in a couple of weeks."

With that, Raymond's display went dark, and then came up on the Command and Control Center. The activity was frantic as orders were given to properly monitor every event that could be tracked.

Volcanoes along the Pacific Rim were erupting and spewing tons of material into the atmosphere. As if the earth was being squeezed, every active volcano began to erupt. New volcanoes were forming in the Antarctic and super storms were being generated around each mass. This signaled the beginning of the event that Raymond had warned of: it even accelerated the pressure on the earth as more particulate weighted down on a fragile planet. Panic started to filter its way to the evacuation zones, and all transportation ceased. Earthquakes shook the planet on a global scale…those who were in the safety zones would be the sole survivors of earth's greatest disaster.

CHAPTER 4

Richard and Maryann Steve had been in Maine for the past couple of months. Richard helped secure his sister's home against the incoming storms and Maryann spent most of her time preparing food and supplies.

Richard had two good helpers, Todd and Chris Deveau. His nephews were handsome young men in their early twenties. Although their knowledge of construction and buildings was only basic, Richard had an opportunity to teach them everything he knew, and once the house was secure, Todd and Chris were well versed in construction techniques.

On the morning of August 13th, 2030, Richard grabbed his coffee and went to the front porch overlooking Bar Harbor. For the past few weeks the morning sunrises were spectacular with a big red sun rising from the ocean, but this morning something seemed out of place. He went to the door and opened it slowly, whispering "Maryann, come out here and see this."

Maryann emerged carrying her own cup of coffee, expecting to join her husband on the front porch for a beautiful sunrise and some affection. At first she saw only Richard, staring at the sunrise; then she looked up as well. She dropped her coffee.

"Oh my God! *Oh My God!*" terror had filled her voice; her eyes started to well up and she felt a burning sensation in the back of her throat.

"What is that?"

She saw a blood red line along the horizon that looked as if it was pulsing towards them. Above the line, the crimson sun was dipping below the horizon and then appearing again, doing jumping jacks on a celestial scale and defying logic. The knowledge that the sun rises in the east and moves west across the sky to the west in a slow, straight line was now starkly contradicted by what was happening before their eyes.

Richard could not believe what he was watching. He was a trained engineer, he knew physics and mechanics, and this could not be possible.

"What the hell is going on?" Richard said. "This is not right, how can the sun be moving up and down?" Richard could not comprehend what he was seeing, yet he knew the answer to the question somewhere in his brain. He and Maryann stood there and watched the sun rise and set for about fifteen minutes before the sun was fully visible in the sky. It looked as if it was bouncing in the early morning sky. Richard also noticed that the red haze was getting thicker and darker, the aura around the sun was a dark black ring and seemed to be getting thicker.

Richard ran into the house and yelled for everyone to get up. Maryann went to the kitchen to put on more coffee and prepare breakfast. She had a feeling this might be an important breakfast, so she set about making it a feast.

Everyone had gathered on the porch to witness what was happening. Todd stared at the sun for a couple of minutes and then with a blank stare looked at Richard. "Uncle, what's going on?"

Richard paused for a moment and finally figured out what his response would be. "Well I think the planet is wobbling on its axis. That would make the sun appear as if it is bobbing up and down in the sky. I'm not sure what would cause this, but I think the dirt in the atmosphere might have something to do with it. Think of the earth as a spinning top—if you throw some putty on it, the top will not spin in a uniform manner, but wobble. That is what's happening now. I don't know what the putty is, but I think it might be volcanoes."

Todd could grasp that concept, although he really did not comprehend what it would mean for his family' survival. Richard, on the other hand, did understand that what they were witnessing was what he could only describe as the end of the days.

"Come inside everyone and have breakfast." called Maryann. "I've got everybody's favorites prepared, and even maple syrup for Grandpa."

Richard was the last to enter the house: as he closed the door, he noticed the tide going out in the harbor, something that did not normally occur so rapidly—it moved gently, but Richard knew that it would not return in the same fashion. He remained quiet as he sat and prayed with his family, giving thanks for breakfast and asking the Lord to watch over them in these troubled times.

The conversation over breakfast centered on how things came to be: the changes to the planet, the evacuations, and the state of preparations carried out.

"Uncle Richard," said Todd, "do you really think that we can stop any damage from the weather?"

Richard looked around the table; he sensed that

everyone was hanging on his words. "I think we can stop most of the damage, but I'm not really sure what's coming our way. Information has been scarce, and in the past few weeks everyone has left for the evacuation zones. Todd, I think it's all up to God and his will as to how we make out. I'm sure he will protect his flock, and keep us from harm's way."

Richard knew they wouldn't survive the water, but wanted to keep his family calm and their faith strong. He got up from the table and went to the front porch again.

From this vantage point he could see the ocean acting like a big bucket of water being carried up a hill: the tide would receded and then come rushing back in. He was reminded of the tidal bores he once saw in Nova Scotia. Along the Salmon River, just outside of Truro, people would line the banks to see a six-inch wall of water come rushing up the river. This was one of the few places in the world where you could actually see the tide come in. The wave would make all the twists and turns along the river bank and then pass. Then the water would rise in the river until it reached the top of the banks in a very short period of time. When the tide went out, it wouldn't drop as fast, but it was noticeable and you could tell at low tide something powerful had happened. There was no vegetation on the mud flats, just smooth red mud that was scraped clean twice a day by the powerful Bay of Fundy tides.

The Bar Harbor basin was starting to take on that appearance: the rocky bottom was being replaced with mud, and the water was now a deep brown cloudy color. The tidal action was taking place every hour and it appeared to be getting stronger. Richard was joined by the entire family as they sat and watched the tides ebb and flow. In the middle of the afternoon, the last tidal wave came in from the Atlantic Ocean. It was 10 to 15 feet high and roaring angrily. It came into the mouth of the harbor and took away the light house, then continued through the basin—no boats were left, and most of the wharfs and bridges were gone, but this wall of water kept on moving towards the centre of town. Like a bulldozer, the wall of water hit the remaining buildings with such force that they collapsed, as if someone pulled the bottom floor out from under each building. The wave continued until it stopped at the top of the waterfront business district. Leaving nothing standing, the harbor had doubled in size in a matter of minutes. The water did not recede this time. It slowly settled and remained in the basin, keeping ownership of all the land and buildings it had just claimed.

Richard watched, and could only be a bystander to Mother Nature's fury. When the tides stopped, he could feel the ground starting to vibrate.

"Everyone inside now!" He yelled. "Get to the basement, go go!"

The family scrambled into the basement shelter, in preparation for the next event. Richard was the last to enter the shelter they had constructed. A waterproof, self-contained "bomb" shelter that was built with plans from the early 1960s. At the time those rooms were for nuclear war, but this time the war being waged was a one-sided battle. Earth was going to correct its imbalance.

On the afternoon of August 13th, 2030, planet earth transformed from a wobbling globe into an angry shaking celestial body. The moment had arrived where a complete makeover of the continents and oceans would take place.

West of the San Andreas Fault, the land slid into the Pacific Ocean. Japan, Taiwan, and the Hawaiian islands slipped beneath the Pacific Ocean; any remnants were wiped clean by the tsunami that came from the west coast of the US. The Pacific ring of fire was burning bright and hot, with water temperatures rising a degree an hour. Western Europe was struck by a wall of water 50 meters in height from Greenland's initial violent melt off. The remaining glaciers on Greenland, influenced by the heat of the land, melted into the Atlantic, and the sea level rose an additional sixty meters. Florida, Louisiana, and most of Texas were submerged; the Dead Sea was resurrected and swallowed surrounding countries.

In the course of 12 hours, most of the ice on the planet had liquefied. The faults along the great continental plates had separated and caused some minor earthquakes, which were unexpected at the USGS. Scientists were sure that any movement along the plates would cause massive earthquakes, and widespread damage on a global scale. This was not the case, as the plates separated; any pressure was released by volcanic activity and not through the plates shifting.

At the USGS, Stuart Matheson's team was running data through the super computers. Josh Perry ran one simulation after another: as the senior programmer and analyst he wanted to be sure his data was accurate and verifiable. Josh ran his third scenario and reached for the phone.

"Dr. Matheson? Josh here. I think you should come down here, it looks like things are setting up for the final correction."

"On my way." Stuart started to run to the computer simulation room. He knew that anything Josh put together was very accurate; if he called, the situation was very serious. Stuart came through the security doors to the computer simulation lab, sweat dripping from his brow, his mobile phone still in his hand.

"What'cha got, Josh?"

"Well, I've run the simulation three times based on the data from the birds and sensors, I think that the earth is going to—for lack of a better word—bump back into shape in less than 12 hours."

"Bump?" Stuart looked confused, and couldn't figure out how Josh, a PhD in earth sciences and computer programming could come up with a simple word like bump.

"Yes. If you look at the screens, you'll see that all the continental plates have separated, releasing any pressure. The volcanoes have stopped erupting for the most part, and no new tsunamis are being generated—just the remnants are crossing the oceans now. The seismographic data from all the monitoring stations are now reporting extremely reduced or no activity. I think we are going to have one hell of a ride very soon." Josh sat down in his chair, wiped his glassed on his shirt and repeated, "yep, one hell of a ride, real soon."

"How soon, Josh? You have to be specific! I have to inform Dr. Braemore, we have to get word out for everyone to hang on."

"Well, based on the data and the fact the plates are 6 to 12 miles apart from each other, the flow of the magma under the plates, and the spinning of the planet, I would calculate that in the next eight and a half hours everything is going to bump back into place. The plates will come together again, and the continents will start moving against each other. I figure the earth is going to have one more earthquake of 10 on the Richter scale, and a dozen or so aftershocks from 7 to 9. Indications are that that the geological portion will be over in the next 24 hours, then the meteorological events take over. If we survive the bump, we'll survive anything else that can be thrown at us."

Stuart laid his phone on Josh's desk, then rubbed his temples and took about five seconds to comprehend what Josh was saying., He grabbed his phone off the desk and headed back to his office. On the way, he stopped into the Command Center to advise the duty General of their new findings.

"Come on, come on." Stuart was not used to having Raymond's phone ring more than twice. "Ray, hang on, the big one is coming! I have just sent Josh's findings directly to you. Get the word out, and start praying. It looks like everyone is going on a big ride."

He pressed end on the phone, slumped down in his office chair and started to cry. Dr. Stuart Matheson, Director of the USGS, was finally showing that he was a human after all, and scared to death.

The timing was very accurate. Seven hours and 55 minutes after Stuart called Raymond, the ground started to move. What Stuart noticed was that it was not the classic side to side motion of an earthquake; the motion was more linear and in pulsating motions. He thought it was like one of those moving sidewalks at the airports, but the belts were slipping. There was forward motion, but not steady.

Fifteen minutes after the movement started, there was a massive bump. Everything stopped and flew into the air. Desks, chairs, people, anything that was not bolted down was thrown up at a height of about two feet. Damage was extensive, but not as devastating as a regular earthquake. After the analysis, it was apparent that everything, including the continental plates moved in one motion, and then settled into the new global configuration.

At the Command and Control Center, real time data from the satellites showed the four great continents were isolated by water and Antarctica's land mass was consumed with the run off. The environmental disaster that came from the erasure of the coastal communities caused great concern. Landfills were swamped, buildings were destroyed and anything left behind was tossed around and destroyed by the forces of nature. Tsunamis had been generated and raced across the Pacific, Atlantic and India Oceans at 1000 kilometers an hour. The shorelines were new, and the tsunamis were going to make them pristine, washing everything away, leaving nothing that would show mankind had ever been there.

Everything played out like a fantastic movie. Satellite images showed what looked like moving continents; the ripples of the tsunamis could be seen, washing across every inch of coastline across the globe four and five times. The movement could be felt everywhere. In Utah, a category 5 earthquake lasted for fifty minutes causing some minor damage, but having more effect on peoples' nerves rather than property. Nothing that wasn't tied down was stationary: everything and everyone moved with the planet's ebb and flow.

The big earthquake that lasted fifteen minutes was long enough to ensure total devastation of the affected areas that were along the big fault lines. In the safe zones, people reported having the feeling of falling for what seemed like hours; earthquakes and fires erupted and the emergency crews, already exhausted from the evacuations, were not permitted to intervene. All was left for Mother Nature to rectify. The evacuee camps had become refugee camps now, left to the mercy of the elements yet still standing. The location of the safe zones were accurate almost to the meter. Damage was minor in these areas; the refugees knew of the events taking place, but felt secure enough to venture outside and witness what was happening. The clouds were dark and grey, but no precipitation prevailed. Winds were increasing; no one really noticed the absence of birds in the sky.

There was widespread devastation outside the safety zones. Readings confirmed that the earth's size had increased ten percent, and the reflection of sunlight from the planet had increased, indicating an atmosphere full of clouds and debris. In the middle of the Atlantic Ocean, conditions were right for the formation of a super hurricane. Away from any land now, and waters heated by geothermal activity, conditions were about to produce what scientists called Gaia.

This name was derived from the 1960's Gaia hypothesis that felt the earth was a living entity. It lived and breathed in harmony with all creatures and matter. The Earth was alive and Gaia was her name. The balance of nature was attributed to Gaia. If things die, Gaia resurrected them in other forms. If you harmed the earth, then Gaia would take out her anger and restore the balance by any means necessary. It was this mythology that the scientists based the name of the hurricane on, and the fact that the hurricane was going to help restore the balance of nature.

The cyclonic action of Gaia had started to move debris towards its center. At first indications were that the center of the storm would grow over a couple of days, but in reality, Gaia formed as fast as a tornado in the great plains of the United States of North America. As Gaia churned in the central Atlantic Ocean, cyclonic winds reached 400 even 500 miles an hour; tons of matter was drawn into the centre of the storm and then expelled into outer space.

This matter, rising to a height of 500 kilometers, formed a ring around the planet, the ring grew in density and color. The grays and reds of fresh volcanic ash combined to make an orange band surrounding earth: 50 kilometers wide and 5 kilometers thick, it was apparent that as the atmosphere cleared, the ring was solidifying; this ring was to be a new permanent feature of the third plant from the sun.

Winds on the land were reaching 70 and 80 miles an hour; above that, they were approaching 1000 miles an hour near the jet stream. Clouds were starting to look like jet streams themselves as the upper winds accelerated and moved towards the super hurricane in the Atlantic.

Jenna and Steve were in their shelter, still shaking from the quake and bump. Their shelter survived, as did they, much to their relief.

"Jenna, I'm going outside to survey the damage."

"Not without me you're not." Jenna quickly grabbed a sweater, and then Steve's arm. "If you think that I'm going to stay here alone you've got another thing coming, mister."

Steven chuckled. "Ok, hang on tight, let's go."

Steve opened the door, expecting to see everything in piles of rubble, but that was not the case. All of the buildings in his block were standing. Nothing looked unusual, except the color. There was a reddish glow over everything. Steve looked up to see big red clouds with no features, all heading east. They appeared to be picking up speed. Jenna picked up on the sound.

"Steve, do you hear that?"

To human observers on the ground, the angry howling of the winds high up made things surreal. Gaia was growing, and most of the material she inhaled was being expelled. The band around the equator was now casting an opaque shadow around the equatorial region of the earth. This area, once the hottest on earth, was now starting to cool down; as it was the catalyst for some of the planet's weather, there would be no energy to kick up any storms. Off of the Western coast of Africa, where Atlantic hurricanes formed, the sea temperature was now decreasing. It was predicted to fall ten degrees by the end of the year. Not enough to generate storms and not enough to fuel hurricanes, it would become a vital part of a new convection engine that would drive the earth's weather for many centuries. To the west, the Pacific basin and Indian Ocean wouldn't generate typhoons and cyclones.

Although the convergence zones were still in place from the earth's rotation, the sea temperatures have dropped below 27.5C and the formation of these storms is unlikely. Also, with this cooling band around the equator, the major ocean currents started shifting as well. The famous Gulf Stream split, moving warmer water to the polar and equatorial regions. Fish stocks and migratory patterns of sea animals have been altered and will have a devastating effect on stocks, until evolution can rectify the matter. History has shown that evolution can adapt very fast, and left alone will balance out once again. The commercial fisheries have been wiped out: by the time they are rebuilt, ocean life will have been undisturbed for decades.

Gaia churned in the Atlantic Ocean for three days and then as fast as it formed, the biggest hurricane ever recorded on planet Earth dissipated and the clouds broke away. The winds calmed and the loud sounds of the high levels winds faded.

Steve ventured outside, this time leery of the environment. He was greeted with sunshine and calm winds. He looked up and saw no clouds, just a deep blue sky; to the south he could see a ring along the horizon, deep red with clean edges, hanging just above the skyline.

"Jenna, you've got to see this. It's beautiful."

Jenna made her way to the door, stepped next to

Steve and looked up. Birds were flying again and in massive flocks. They seemed to be searching for something.

"I wonder if they're hungry?" quipped Steve. "We haven't seen anything flying in a week or so."

The Mars colony finally made contact with Command and Control on Earth on August 15th. Reporting from Mars, C&C learned that the Earth was bigger, the rotation faster, and the ring of the Earth was a very distinguishable feature that made it even more beautiful. The Moon base made contact a day afterward and sent back high resolution pictures of the reformed landscape. Earth was a deeper shade of blue now, with larger oceans and only four continents masses. One gigantic ring circled the planet: North America, South America, Asia and Africa were all that remained. The location of the safe zones was in the middle of each, and mankind now had to make some decisions on how to repopulate this newly reformed planet.

The colonies on the Moon and Mars were self-sufficient, and would remain in place while the representatives of each zone gathered in Utah for Earth's first and most important meeting: how to govern the planet, forge ahead, and survive the changes that will affect every living being. Earth's magnetic fields were still in place, and the Global Positioning System would have to be recalibrated, but it was still functioning. Taking into account the loss of land and cities, the database of existing GPS coordinates would have to be changed. Command and Control started to work on this immediately after the global reset. The magnetic fields pointing to the North and South Poles had shifted and were symmetrical with the exact top and bottom of the planet. Earth had shifted on its axis and now rotated square on with the sun. There would be no more seasons, no more cyclical weather patterns like the rainy seasons in Asia, or blizzards in Siberia. For changes in climate, one would have to go North or South, depending where you were in relation to the equator. The temperate zone, formerly Tropic of Cancer, was now a very comfortable area to live in: temperatures ranged from 30 to 40 degrees Celsius in the day and 15 to 25 at night. North from this was 20 to 30, and the top of the continent had a temperature range of minus 20 to minus 10. Weather was dictated again by the oceans, and became predictable as sunshine in the daylight hours, precipitation in the overnight and back to sunshine. The major currents that sparked violent weather in the ocean and atmosphere were gone. There was just enough energy to maintain the environment as it stood. Whether this would continue was anyone's guess, but for now it made the rebuilding of society easier.

Flight was possible again, and the representatives were called to Utah for a September 15th meeting. The Global Civilization had to have a governing body to help mankind survive and evolve. The problems of the day were where to locate two billion people, how to feed them, how to give them purpose and how to grow as a society now free of the bonds of currency and religion. Raymond conferred with his staff and called together some of the best surviving economic and philosophical minds to lay out the framework for this new venture for mankind. Simon Gross, leading economy professor with Harvard University; Roy Davies, literature guru on the past, present and future of currencies; Gena Regeas, Doctor of Russian Economics and author of high finance thrillers; and of course Sebastian Gore, grandson of Albert Gore, Academy award winner for the first mass media warning about Global Warming. Sebastian took up his grandfather's fight and had been instrumental in predicting the events that unfolded in the past few months. Sebastian and Raymond were close friends and spent many hours discussing solutions to the problems that were unfolding. The five people who would create the ideas that would lead to the next step in mankind's journey were to meet in the next 24 hours. Helicopters and jet planes were dispatched. The meeting room was prepared by Jocelyn and her counterparts with huge white boards, laptop computers and video cameras that covered every angle. No idea or suggestion could be lost; technology would ensure that this marathon session was recorded for all to witness.

The participants arrived, eager to get started. Roy Davies had foretold of the virtual currency revolution; he predicted that cash would no longer be needed, with the Internet invading every aspect of life. Banks, stock markets, and households were connected. Dollars went from payrolls directly into accounts and hand held devices, which were used by everyone to transfer funds for payment. Roy had imagined almost every conceivable method of moving money around, but could not forsee the elimination of currency all together. His philosophy was strong, and accurate right up until the beginning of the next phase, which was something he could not predict or fathom. But he had had time to think, and would bring some interesting ideas to the table. His counterpart and nemesis Gena Regeas arrived at the meeting center around the same time. Gena was responsible for putting the Russian economy back on track and eliminating the double digit inflation that plagued the Russians since the mid 90s in the 20th century. Her ideas for monitoring money were based on some of Roy's work, but melded into her unique way. Every citizen of Russia was given a debit card, and all the banks were merged into one. There was no avenue for money laundering, no way for organized crime to hide their gains from the black market, so the second economy of Russia was abandoned and replaced with legitimate business transactions. Inflation sank to a new low of three percent, and stayed there right up to the day the monetary system died. Russians were able to hang on to more funds, and the lifestyle of the middle class was greatly improved. The free market system in Russia was working, bread lines disappeared: every citizen had a fair chance to accumulate disposable income, and use it for life's luxuries like video screens and computers. Russia embraced technology, eliminated the "made in Russia" mentality and started to import and export goods at an outstanding rate. The Ford manufacturing system was introduced, and the technology for clean vehicles was shared worldwide. Ford licensed its technology to Russia's Lada Company, and orders were on demand. Production was up and Russia's vast natural resources enabled them to export vehicles on order to countries all over the world. Shipping vehicles by rail, sea and road was easy, since Russia was the middle ground between China and Europe. All the while, exporting vehicles and other products kept Russia's economy strong.

Simon Gross had some preconceived notions about a cashless society: he saw every person carrying an identity card that would serve as the main transaction vehicle. These cards would be loaded by the owners nightly from the internet in their homes, or for big ticket items, could be loaded from a banking terminal at a store or a street corner. His method was not far from the overall goal of eliminating the accumulation of cash for the common person, and accounting for the acquisition of goods and services. He had thought of a credit-for-work system, but did not think it could ever come to be. Simon's methodology would be the basis for the policies about to be constructed. The main hurdle was how to account for every man, woman and child who required products to survive.

Simon conferred with Sebastian on how to accomplish this, and Sebastian had some strong opinions, mostly that everyone should be treated as an equal regardless of age, sex, religion, or background. The planet and living in harmony with it was a priority to ensure that nothing like this would ever happen again. Mankind had to survive within the constraints that Mother Nature placed upon it. The identity cards would have to be ecofriendly yet durable. Food would be grown, and harvested in the same manner. Manufacturing of products would be on a need basis, and long production lines pumping out excessive articles would be a thing of the past. The old society norms of got to have, like to have, need to have would be replaced with need to have, and will need to have. Existence will be minimalistic at best for the next few centuries. The goals of shelter, food, and something to occupy one's time have to be addressed. Shelter would be classified as a warm, energy-efficient place to live. Each person would have a private space, and the common areas would be combined to make it more efficient. The days of a two- or three-story house were gone. For the sake of individuality, the new designs could be any shape, but there would be a specific number of rooms, all heated by the same method and all conforming to the new standards. Mankind had to rebuild, but the technology was in place to allow for some individuality, while maintaining the strictest guidelines.

The five made their way into the main conference room of Command and Control. Each took a seat at the table and started up their computers, video screens and communication devices. Water was poured at each seating place, and a pitcher was left with each participant. If they required more water, they would turn on a switch on the side of the pitcher and the water would instantly become cold and ready to drink. Once they poured their glass of water, the switch was thrown to stop the chilling of the contents. This was one of the new products that caused the manufacture of ice cubes to stop, thereby eliminating the need for creating more pollution to cool the water. Devices like the pitcher were created out of necessity, but now would become mass produced for every household. Storing drinks in a refrigerator took up space, and since this was no longer required the storage space inside the units decreased, along with the energy consumption.

Raymond took a sip of water and was the first to

speak. "I would like to welcome you all to this historic event. We have been charged by the survivors to begin to rebuild the infrastructure of civilization. We have simple goals, and complex methods to consider. The main goal right now is how do we eliminate the need for currency? Secondary goals, what does one do if they do not have to work to earn a living? How do we keep track of an individual's mental growth? If no one has to work, how do we supply consumers with products they require? These are the questions that have to be resolved before we leave this complex and start rebuilding. I'll bring you up to date on the status of the planet and the survivors, while you ponder your presentations. The terms of this meeting are as follows: one, everyone gets a chance to speak; two, a vote on anything must pass by eighty percent, or four out of five delegates. If the vote is lower, the author of the motion will have a chance to explain, and the challenger will have a rebuttal. The vote will then be retaken, and in the event of a stalemate, I will intervene and cast a final vote." What Ray was telling the delegates is that they must work together to come up with solutions, and he would have the final say on each issue. His confidence in the parties almost guaranteed that it would not come to that.

"And Three: we will take a twenty minute break each two hours to stretch, and clear our heads. Any requirements for food or beverages will be met by one of my assistants. After twelve hours, we will take a four hour break for some rest and then dive back into the process. This will repeat itself until we are finished and have a rock-solid plan to present to the general assembly. Any questions?" There was a pause in the room—no one had any questions, they all looked like they were race horses at the gate, ready to jump onto the track and start the race of their lives.

Simon started the debate. "Mr. Chairman, and esteemed collogues, we are here to accomplish something that only a year ago mankind could not comprehend. The economies of the world's nations were strong, and on track. The GDP of each country was stable, and a truly free trade atmosphere was beginning to take root. The Europeans were trading with the Eastern nations, and tariffs were nonexistent. I was sure that as consumers and countries realized the benefits of working and selling together, more jobs were being created as markets expanded. Take, for example, the Lada company: not only did they turn out a fine product, but the on-demand manufacturing process ensured customer loyalty, repeat business, and fewer consumer complaints. The momentum of this manufacturing process was just starting to take hold when everything had to be abandoned to ensure the survival of the species. There are factories still intact at all four corners of the globe, the infrastructure for power distribution remains, thanks to the foresight of the utilities to sever the connections to the areas of total loss. For the first time in human history, we have an abundance of resources that cannot be used up by the two billion surviving members of the human race. The problem that we are now faced with is how to best utilize the resources with the talent? I am sure that there are tradespeople, engineers, sales people and professionals whose dream was to become wealthy and live in the proverbial home with the white picket fence. Europeans were envious of the North American way of life and were just starting to taste it, with all the excess that money brings. How do we tell them they no longer have to accumulate wealth? How do we tell the North Americans that they no longer have any wealth? The monetary system was presented as a big "X", North America through Australia, as the "haves", and South America and Asia as the "have nots"!

"I'll let you think about that while I present my answer to you." Simon stood up and put a graphic on the video display of the current land masses of the newly reformed Earth. Superimposed over each continent was a box labeled A through D. "What we have to do is divide the work required to sustain the population, and then move the population to each area of expertise. We are going to inform the population that they no longer have to work for a living, but rather work for the improvement of life on the planet. Our opportunity to take an inventory of each individual's skills has never been better, with the population so concentrated in four separate places. Language and religious barriers will fall, and the only unknown is preconceived notions of other races. This discrimination may have been eliminated during the month of hell we all experienced. People were working side by side, comforting each other, and taking a noticeable interest in the survival of their fellow being. I'm sure the Catholics prayed to their God and the Muslims to theirs, but near the end it became apparent they were praying to the same entity. I have seen this happen with my own eyes in Russia: one of the mostly British camps joined with an Italian camp and then they all held hands one evening. They were joined by camps from Gaza and India, and around midnight, four of the world's biggest religions became a group of human beings, oblivious of religion, and caring for the well being of each other. I am sure that this was just one scene that took place all over the world."

Simon felt sure that his hypothesis about the melding of religions was just one factor that would make this transition easier. "I feel that we have to draft a Global Constitution, but not thousands of words, and clauses that can be interpreted any which way, rather a document that outlines each person's rights as an individual. The Global Constitution must preserve an individual's right to religion, security, and freedom, and at the same time protect the society we are creating."

Dr. Braemore raised an eyebrow; an epiphany was coming to light. "What if we said that each citizen of the world community has the right to exist in harmony with everyone? I mean we have to allow individuals to pray to their respective gods, but we do not have to have that god pressed upon us. Groups are free to practice their religions, and citizens are free to join what every religion they wish." Dr. Braemore saw that he broke Simon's stride, "I'm sorry Simon, please continue."

Simon nodded. "Thank you, Raymond. This is an open forum for discussion and policy making, so please, anyone feel free to jump into the thought process; but not too fast." Simon noted that everyone nodded. "The first draft about religion I would say is near completion. Simple, direct and there is not a lot of wording for misinterpretation. I'm sure you would all agree with Dr. Braemore's thoughts on keeping an individual's rights first priority. A lot of people are wondering what they are going to do now. I think that if they knew whatever they do, it is proclaimed as a right, and then they won't worry as much." Simon paused to look at his notes. "I seem to have gotten off track, albeit a good sidetrack; one issue down, one still being worked on." Simon looked around the room. "Sebastian, would you like to pick up from me? I'm sure you agree that this forum has dropped all formalities now, and we are getting down to working with ideas. I know you and I have had the chance to talk many times and I think we're on the same page."

Sebastian Gore had many doodles on his papers, designs for identity cards, community layouts, the center of government, all drawn with some purpose, and all connected with lines. Sebastian stood, held up his paper and said on a soft voice, "I think this is the blueprint for our society." Handing the paper to an aide, it was scanned and put on everyone's personal video display. "From the beginnings of the identity card, issued to every man, woman and child, all the way up through the seat of government, we have to keep it simple. It is my belief that the current government structure that was enacted before this crisis is the one that should remain in place. This relieves us of the necessity of setting up a new government, trying to explain to someone new how this all took place, and what the purpose is. It has never been done before, and since many of the governing bodies no longer have land to govern, it only makes sense to keep to the status quo and build on that." Everyone in the room nodded, except for Raymond; he had just been given the top job, and he was not sure he wanted to keep it. "Raymond, I can appreciate your apprehension, but all that I ask, I mean all that we ask, is you give it a chance, see what this will look like at the end of the day." Raymond then nodded in approval.

"I'd like to start by introducing the concept of no money." Sebastian said, he then emptied his pockets of the loose change that had been there for the past six months. He giggled. "I'm sorry—old habits are hard to break. I can grasp the concept of no money, but cannot let go of the habit of putting my change on the night stand every night." The room exploded in laughter.

Raymond knew this was not a very funny joke, but was just the relief everyone was looking for, the ice breaker if you will, that got these people really working as a team. "Ok everyone, empty out your pockets, and we'll put all the money in a jar. It might be a symbol some day, but today it is just a worthless jar, full of metal and paper."

Sebastian understood what was being done and said: that jar may someday end up in a museum as the "Last Jar of Cash" ever collected. "Thanks for contributing to my pension fund." More snickers. "But let's move on. Currently in Salt Lake City, Moscow, Shanghai, and Brazilia there are facilities to print credit cards. I suggest we put in an order for two billion cards, and start to collect data for identity cards."

The papers on Sebastian's desk were now divided into neat piles, each one representing a continent, and the basic design for the identity questionnaire was intact. "Since most countries issued some form of identification, we can utilize the Internet and data storage we set up to retrieve a lot of information; but this will have to be verified, and the former illegal aliens will have to give us accurate information. They will need to know that there will be no reprisals; everyone that survived is a new citizen of the world community. We have check in stations already set up in the major camps, so this should not be too hard to accomplish." Sebastian paused for a moment, hoping that Raymond or someone would interject.

"There are questions no one has answered yet: production, acquisition, and motivation." There was a long pause, almost too long. Sebastian started to become nervous; then Gena Regeas spoke up.

"I think that Roy Davies should address what you are thinking, Sebastian. We are all thinking the same thing. Do we still have jobs? Do we have the latitude to acquire anything we want? What is the motivation to do something for nothing? Perhaps that last questions is not accurate, but I think you know what I mean. There are some things in the world that need to be done, and they are menial tasks. Poor people were motivated to perform these tasks to survive; now they do not have to." Gena sat down quickly.

Roy hesitated, but then grabbed a glass of ice

water, drank it down slowly, almost as if it was his first drink in months; he wanted to savor the moment. "Gena, esteemed partners, this is the question: what do I have to do today so that I contribute to the survival of my fellow human beings?" A long pause ensued. Roy poured more water, looked around the room, and took another slow drink. "You see around us now aides, technicians, and photographers. Has anyone asked about money for their job? What about the delegates? Do we get a stipend? Do we get our expenses paid for? Since there is in effect no more money, then there is no more perceived motivation to perform a job. But what are you all doing here? The answer is simple: we enjoy doing what we do. The aides enjoy making sure our documents are well prepared and we are looked after, so that the only thing we have to concentrate on is their well being. The photographers enjoy documenting everything for the record, ensuring that what goes on here is accurate, fair, and for our well being. Same goes for the technicians, the volunteers who helped build the shelters, and feed the millions; it was all done for our well being.

Roy knew he was on camera, and he liked it. Raymond knew that Roy was show-boating, but let him carry on, since it was making such a dramatic point. Roy sat down and drank some more water. "What we have to get our society to do is work for their well being. People need to have some structure in their lives; I don't think we are ready to fall into despair becoming a world of couch potatoes. We need to work at the jobs we had, unless the industry does not exist; then we need to train to work at other jobs. The market for financial analysts is gone, but the market for teachers, engineers, and researchers has just expanded. This cannot be accomplished overnight, but it will happen. Until then we have to make do with what we have, and know. Expand our horizons, and really, really make sure we accomplish things that we want to do to ensure our well being." It was with that brief speech: Raymond, Sebastian, Gena, and Simon stood and applauded Roy. He remained standing, still drinking from his glass of water, and basking in the accolades. Raymond gave him about two minutes, and then hammered a gavel on the desk, "order, order please" he shouted. "We need to continue on, people, we need to figure out how we are going to put this in print." Raymond knew he had their attention, "What are we going to do for those who do not know what they want to do? Or the school children when they graduate?"

"Easy," said Simon. "They will have the opportunity to choose. They will have a list of occupations that tie into their attributes, and from that list they will start to train and develop their skills into a viable contributors to society."

Mumbles of agreement sounded throughout the room. Jocelyn Burris-Stone had to agree with this and spoke up, much to the surprise of the delegates and the amusement of Raymond.

"I like that thought. I mean after all, I've been Raymond's assistant for many years, and really enjoy my job." She shifted in her chair. "If someone asked me why I do what I do, I would have to say for the sheer enjoyment. I like making travel arrangements, proofreading papers, and running Raymond's life." This brought laughter to the room. "No. What I mean is facilitating everything necessary for Raymond to concentrate on his duties, and not have to worry about his laundry, plane tickets, or hotels. Making sure that his house is properly cared for, and that when he takes time off it is really time off, not a working vacation."

"You really enjoy what you do?" Simon inquired. "I mean, did you feel that you had to get paid for the work you did?"

"Not really. I did like the pay, but it was not my

motivation. I actually looked forward to coming into work, and the adventures that I was going to send Raymond on." With that Simon knew he was on the right track. His biggest worry was how to relay this message to the masses: what are they going to think? How are they going to react?

Raymond banged the gavel again. "I would like to suggest that we take a break to formulate our thoughts and get some of this on paper for formalization." He looked around the room; people were already starting to huddle into groups. "Any opposed?" No one said anything; the gavel came down again. "A two hour break it is." Raymond motioned to Jocelyn to follow him, and they left the meeting room to go to the gardens.

The gardens were actually a big arboretum that had once been the Brigham Young University's pride and joy. Students practiced their craft by creating spaces where people could enjoy the flora, and not really feel like they were in a city. The foliage was so thick that the noise of the city could not be heard, although now that was a moot point now since no cars, trains, or planes were permitted to move except by special permit. Raymond found an area that had a fountain that resembling a dolphin, surrounded by red brick footstones and lush green grass. The benches were all crescent shaped and facing the fountain. The solar engine that ran this display was expertly hidden behind a row of red-leaved bushes, and Raymond thought that with all that has taken place, this seemed like the most peaceful area to be. Raymond and Jocelyn sat down.

"Jocelyn, did you really mean all those things you said back there? Is my life so hectic that I need to be organized by someone else just to function?

"Yes, Raymond. I did mean all those things, but I also do not want you to get depressed. I would do what I do for anyone, but I really enjoy doing it for you. You're not a mess, but you are human, and cannot be expected to funnel and direct all the information coming at you, then try to fit personal time into everything. They made you the leader, and in some ways you are the first President of the New World, even though you have been tasked to be the architect of the next phase of mankind. I don't think that the other leaders had gave any thought to survival; I'm sure they were all thinking that this was the end of civilization." Raymond agreed.

"I did not accept the position on a permanent basis, but I think it is going to work out that way. I hope that in ten or twenty years, we can elect a new leader, for the next generation. Bureaucracy is about to change."

Jocelyn ordered some lunch from her tablet, and also made sure Raymond ordered from his. "I do sometimes feel like your mother, though. It's a good thing you're potty trained." Raymond and Jocelyn shared a good laugh over that comment just as their lunch arrived. Ray stopped the waiter as he turned to leave.

"Excuse me, can I ask you a frank and personal question?" The waiter, not missing a beat, making sure everything was in order, said with a grin, "Sure, Doctor. You can ask me anything."

"I was wondering, since everything is provided for you now, your family is taken care of, everyone eats well, and you have shelter and warmth, why do you still come to work?"

"Tough question; but not that tough. My name is Wayne Votour, Doctor Braemore. I have been a cook and waiter here at the University for the past thirty years. I came here to further my culinary skills, take some classes in business management and hope to open my own restaurant in Salt Lake City some day."

"Please, Wayne, call me Raymond."

"Ok, Raymond." Wayne felt very uncomfortable

calling such a distinguished man by his first name. He had been brought up to respect those in power, the people he would be working for. What he failed to realize was the new order of things now.

Raymond could sense the uncertainty in Wayne's voice, the nervous shiver that signaled that he thought it was wrong to use first names.

"Wayne, please do not be offended or feel obligated to call me by Doctor, or Mr. Braemore. I know that you and I have both passed the point where neither one of us is better than the next person. You are a great cook, I burn water. I am a troubleshooter to the world's problems, but do not have the richness that you do."

"Thank you Raymond, I must apologize. It is going to take a lot of practice to get used to the new order. To answer your question, it's simple really. I came here to prepare myself for the world, was offered a chef's position and fell in love with the challenges, and the University.

I love what I do. Sure, the hours might not be as short as I would like them to be, but after an eighteen hour day, all the plates come back clean and I can't think of anything more fulfilling and satisfying I'd rather be doing."

Wayne looked at Raymond with conviction,

Raymond could see it, that slight swell in the chest, the head cocked higher and the wry little smile. Raymond was looking at a man who really did love his job. "Thanks Wayne. You've given me the answer I was looking for, and I am now proud to say that I know Chef Wayne Votour. Thank you for the lunch, and all the best to you and your family."

Wayne instinctively took one last look around to make sure everything was alright and took his leave. "The same to you Raymond. Thank you for saving my life."

Jocelyn saw Raymond's reaction, and she knew he had something. There was a spark in his eyes that was not going to go out. The old adage that 'you can hear the wheels turning' was a perfect fit right now. Raymond did not say anything for the next hour, but looked like he wanted to. They got up from their bench, took their waste to the biodegradable bins and headed back inside the conference center.

Chapter 5

The words of the proposed document started were now on everyone's video display. They were bold and clear.

As the surviving members of the human race, be it resolved that we are now part of a single community. We will strive to live by these words and develop as a whole for the betterment of mankind.

Clause 1.   Everyone has the right to exist. To respect others rights, and be respected by others. Everyone will have the right to be a citizen of the Global Community.

Clause 2.   Everyone will have an identity card to obtain goods and services necessary to facilitate the quality of life that we have come to expect. Non-Citizens will have privileges severely reduced.

Clause 3.   No one will have individual access to the means to cause harm to another person.

Only the police, military personnel, and professional hunters will be permitted weapons.

Clause 4. Every Citizen will have the right of individual freedom of religion. Recruiting, forcing, or subverting an individual to adopt a religion that they have not chosen by free will is not permitted. Violators will have Citizen status revoked.

Clause 5. Every Citizen will have the right to choose an occupation of their desire, the right to excel in their profession and the right to cease or change their occupations at the time of their choosing. From 2030 until 2050, occupations may be based on attributes necessary for survival of the human race.

Clause 6. Crimes against Citizens, humanity or the environment will be dealt with in a just and fair manner by a tribunal of elected peers. If found guilty of a crime, Citizen status will be revoked.

Clause 7. Every Citizen regardless of age will have the right to go back to school.

Clause 8. Healthcare academics and researchers

	will be given access to the world's information and research on disease and cancers.
Clause 9.	*No one will be refused any type of health care.*
Clause 10.	*The current government will remain in effect until 2040, at which time an extension of 10 years may be enacted, or until a general election can take place. Government officials will be team leaders in their respective communal areas.*
Clause 11.	*All expenditures from identity cards will be tracked for the lifetime of the card holder. Unusual activity will be investigated and rectified.*
Clause 12.	*The Global Community leaders will meet once a year in Utah to give status and updates on progress.*
Clause 13.	*Every Citizen will have access to the Global Internet.*

Sebastian let everyone read the text. "The idea for this document was to make it short and not open to too much interpretation. After all, there are still going to be lawyers, and they will want to issue challenges. However, the judicial tribunals are made up of members who wrote this document and swore an oath to it. I don't think there will be a problem for at least twenty years." Closing his video screen tablet, Simon leaned back in his chair and stretched his arms out.

"I think we did one hell of a job, all things considered. We had the easy part; relaying the message is going to be harder."

Robert knew this. "What we have here is a new twist on an old idea: Socialism, albeit modified to eliminate the class structures that came from the experiments in the 20th century. I think we have to make it clear that humanity needs to have specific duties covered, and then citizens can expand their horizons. The big difference as I see it is that we are not working for the state, but rather working for the species, growing the species, and fostering an environment where we can eliminate the corruption and deviations from the previous systems."

Robert looked around the room, and what he saw amazed him. Everyone working for a common cause, brought together by a disaster that could have pushed mankind back to the proverbial Stone Age, now writing a new chapter in mankind's development. He had to prepare for the Global Assembly, and explain in detail the context and the will of the new Global Community Writ.

Steve and Jenna were in Utah during the event. They stayed in one of the shelters and helped out with the distribution of food and medicine. Jenna volunteered at the Red Cross center in her block. Her training was put to good use to catalog and maintain records of everything that went through the center. Steve's paramedical abilities were beneficial during the earthquakes. Although no serious injuries occurred, it was traumatic for everyone. The ground did not stop shaking for days on end, and many people had minor injuries.

Situated in their two-room shelter, comfortably laid out with the kitchen and living area combined, a single bathroom with shower and two bed rooms, the setting was sparse, yet livable. After things settled down, Steve and Jenna were contemplating what was next.

"I'm not sure what we should do now," Steve said. "We've been here for few months, and whenever I ask if we can leave, I never get a straight answer."

"Where would you go?" Jenna seemed confused and rather shocked that Steve intended to leave. "Our homes are gone, and the east coast is now along the Mississippi."

"Oh I don't know. But I would like to get away from the crowds, stake out a new claim and begin to rebuild my life—ours, if you would like to come along." Jenna blushed. Even though she and Steve had been roommates since they arrived at the shelters, there had been no intimacy. Just comforting moments, when it all seemed like the end was near, the sky was black and the ground would not stop shaking. For Steve to ask Jenna to accompany him to a new life was comforting and flattering. Jenna felt closeness to Steve that can only be fostered at the time of a traumatic event; whether it would last was anyone's guess.

"I heard that there was going to be an announcement in the next week or so on what is expected of us." Steve said. "Some of the rumors are that we are all going to be placed in work camps and start to rebuild the cities. Others have said that we are going to be let loose and have to forge for ourselves like the pioneers of the early eighteenth century. Honestly I'm not sure what to make of it. I'm sure Dr. Braemore has a grand plan, but I have no idea how he is going to implement it. There are some two billion survivors in the world: how is he going to ensure that they get fed, have sustainable living conditions, and enough money to live on? Wall Street, Bay Street, London's FTSE, and Japan's Nikkei, were wiped out, but what does that mean? No more money? Then how do we buy food, clothing and shelter?"

Jenna could hear the panic starting in Steve's voice.

"Steve," she said calmly, "there is a plan, which I'm sure has been well thought out. The human race started out with sticks and stones, and not much knowledge of the world around them; today we have a vast knowledge of the planet and technological wonders that were designed to make out lives better. Surely we, as a race, can put this knowledge to use and build on what we had and what we know."

Steve acknowledged Jenna's statements and started to calm down a little. The prospect of starting all over was daunting, but he knew in his mind that with Jenna at his side, they could make it work. Word of the general leaders' meeting on September 15th spread throughout the camps and all populations were gathering at the information centers and online for this historical meeting. Jenna and Steve sat in their kitchen with a computer tuned to the broadcast, as did most of the surviving population. On the video screen people could see the leaders of former countries, and the Executive Director of the Global Community, Dr. Braemore, started the meeting.

"Citizens of the planet Earth, I welcome you to a new age, a fresh start here in the Global Community." Applause erupted from the assembly, and cheers went out across the world.

"We have survived a disaster some would have called an extinction event. We have lost many close and dear friends, and all our hearts carry the sorrow and pain of the loss. The population of the planet is slightly over two billion now, and those who did not survive will always be remembered as the last occupants of a very angry planet."

Raymond took a sip of water, removed his glasses and looked directly into the video camera directly in front of him. This gave every person watching the display screens the impression that he was talking directly to them, and Raymond wanted it that way.

"Since we have been forced to embark on a new world order and a system of survival, our team has put together the Global Community Writ. You will see this on your screens now, and be able to read it at any time on-line; it will also be posted at the information stations. We have spent countless hours thinking of ways to repair society's flaws, foster new growth, and most of all ensure humanity's survival and every individual's right to exist. For the next 10 years it is not going to be easy to rebuild our society, but I know that we can do it. We have the ability to learn, and adjust to our conditions. This evolution is humanity's greatest tool, and we can expand upon the ideas, create new ones, and foster an environment where no one will be excluded, everyone will be accountable, and we will know peace and prosperity. We must also take great strides not to repeat the abuse of the planet's resources: since we have already laid the foundation for a green society in recent years, we can just carry on and improve upon the ideas." Raymond paused: he did not want to use rhetoric and long drawn out explanations. He was not a politician, but a leader with a specific agenda and a common goal.

"From the GC Writ you will see that your freedoms and rights are in place, and you will have the opportunity to expand your horizons. Money is no longer necessary!" Again, applause and cheers erupted from every assembly on the planet. Jenna and Steve looked at each other in utter disbelief.

"No money?" Jenna said. "How do we buy the things we need to survive, how do we earn a living, and pay for the things that we need?"

Steve put his arm around her. "Hang on. I'm sure there is more to this."

Raymond knew from the applause and reactions that he had better interrupt the accolades.

"Ladies and Gentlemen, please let me finish. I do not want to cause any panic or stress. There will be no more money, but there will be a system of credit to ensure that everyone can afford whatever they desire to ensure their survival and growth. We are going to issue every citizen an Identity Card utilizing biochip technology, that will enable you to acquire the goods and services you need. For the next 10 years, the Identity Card is all you will need to have access to medical care, groceries, utilities, transportation and housing. Identity card usage will be tracked and accounted for to prevent abuse: if you don't abuse the system, it will reward you with an easier lifestyle, free of the stresses we had before due to the currency system. I am sure that you will adopt this system very rapidly." Raymond then paused to let his statements be absorbed.

"Now, with this new freedom come some responsibilities. We will continue to work and provide services. Former government employees will administrate the new system, the militaries will police the system, emergency services will search for survivors who did not evacuate, and all the other services that we have come to rely on will still be in place. You will work for the benefit of humanity; you will have the opportunity to pursue new opportunities and learning experiences, and fulfill your dreams. For the next 10 years though, we ask that you work in your chosen fields, and strive to improve your position and yourself.

There are those who will try to abuse the system. They will not succeed, and will suffer the consequences of their actions. If you are convicted of a crime, your citizenship and all associated rights will be revoked, and you will be sentenced to work for humanity in a position of the government's choosing. I am sure that without money, crime rates will diminish greatly: the prevention of social crimes will be the focus of the existing police forces. The current laws will remain in effect until they can be researched and reapplied to the new social order.

As for your stay in the evacuation areas, it is now over. Once you have received your Identity Card from your community information center, you are free to move about the country, go back to your homes if they survived, or obtain new housing. Remember we have depleted the food, water and fuel stocks in the countries other than the evacuation areas: if you plan on going any great distance, make sure you are prepared. Your information center can assist you with this. Priorities now are to get the food supplies and building supplies restocked and functioning. Merchants, the information center has all the information you require. If you would like to be a merchant, your information center is the place to go to get set up. I ask that you have a great deal of patience while we jump-start the world again.

We have gone through a lot together over the past six months, and we will go through a lot over the next 10 years, but in the end, we will survive this forced evolution." Raymond stepped back from podium, put his glasses back on and let the air clear.

There was a lot of information in his statement, and even more that was not said. This would be up to the information centers to divulge. The information centers would also answer any questions and issue the Identity Cards. The necessary information had already been downloaded; electronic forms and security information was already on hand for every person who registered to stay at the evacuation areas.

Applicants were lining up almost immediately to receive their information. In Utah, the evacuation centers had begun processing Identity Cards with each center being able to handle about one thousand people an hour. At the rate things were progressing, it would only be a couple of days for the five hundred million people to be processed. Foresight was the key to the efficiency with over five thousand information centers being set up in each evacuation area.

Jenna and Steve were among the first to receive their cards and the first to start preparations to leave Utah. Their plan was to travel north east and setup a homestead along the coast in Vermont. The meteorological information indicated this area is the most desirable location with small variances in temperatures, and close to the expanded Atlantic Ocean. Their vehicle was equipped with a GPS and emergency locator equipment, water and food to last six weeks, and clothing. Maps were given to them with the locations of functioning fuel depots and anticipated markets. All was in order, and on a clear, sunny September morning, they departed for a new adventure in their lives.

CHAPTER 6

As Steve traversed the Interstate system northward to I-80, he noticed how fresh everything seemed. The air was cleaner, the grass was greener and wild life was in abundance.

"I'm glad to see so much survived," he said to Jenna. "Just look at everything. No indication of what happened, just calmness. It's surreal. I'm sure the animals didn't know what was happening."

Jenna agreed. "Um hm." She was focused on the sky. She had never seen it so clear and deep blue in color. There were no jet contrails, no clouds; the sun seemed to be crystal clear, and a very, very bright yellow. "Oh, crap" she said with some frustration, "don't stare at the sun, my mother always said." She then looked over at Steve and blinked forcibly with both eyes crossed. They both started to laugh.

"Let's pull over for a bit." Steve said as he pulled to the side of the road about 50 miles short of Kansas City. "Feel like something to eat or drink?

"I'm fine—in fact, I'm more than fine, I'm excellent. It has been six months of hell, we've survived, and it's not that bad." Steve nodded in agreement. "From what I can see, and the information we have, there is civilization and supplies all the way to White River Junction. That is where we should go."

"White River Junction? What's in White River Junction?" Steve looked at her, surprised: not only did he not know where White River Junction was, he was quite sure Jenna didn't either.

"It is a place I heard of when I was a kid. My parents would talk about their trips to Vermont on the weekends when they were 'a courtin' and how they would go up to the Green Mountains from there and watch the seasons change. They would take day trips all over the countryside, shopping, sightseeing, and 'other things' that left fond memories of Vermont in their minds."

Steve leaned back, "Ah yes…the old covered bridge trick." He looked at Jenna with big eyes. "Seriously, honey, who knows how long these bridges will be here? We should at least make some memories in as many as we can." They both laughed so hard they cried, and Jenna could see that Steve's attitude was beginning to change, from the serious survival mode, to a gentle and funny man she liked very much. She wiped a tear from her eye, then one from Steve's and gave him a gentle kiss. The kiss only lasted a few seconds.

"Thanks, Jenna. I needed that. In fact I need you." His cheeks still wet from laughter, his eyes grew wide and serious. "We've been through a lot together, and I appreciate how you have kept our relationship strictly platonic, and built up a friendship. God knows I wanted to go further, but there were more important things to do." Jenn could only look at Steve. She heard his words, and noticed how his soul was almost visible through his hazel eyes, the outpouring of emotion and sincerity, his gentle touch on her hands.

"We have forged a beautiful friendship through a very difficult time, and things are getting better, our friendship is growing again. I feel as if I have known you all my life, and I feel like I cannot live without you."

Jenn whispered, "Me too. Let's take it slow and build on what we have."

"Agreed," Steve said, "and as we continue this journey, let's keep an open mind, and closer hearts." Both realized that the past six months together had brought them close, and the next few months would surely bind their souls.

"Ok, back into the car, the open road calls!" Steve pointed east, and they got into the car. He checked the fuel gauge and saw that they could go another 300 miles before a fuel stop.

"Next stop St. Louis." He put the car into gear and they headed east on I-80.

They talked about what they wanted to do when they reached White River Junction. They would find a small farm and begin to raise livestock and produce. This would mean registering at the White River Junction Information Center, and selecting their property. The discussions on how to trap the stray animals, care and feed them made the miles pass. A few stops and detours took them to Youngstown, then to the I-80 and Parsippany. From Parsippany they headed north to Albany, along the 87 and 7 to 4, then east to White River Junction.

By the time they were within 40 miles of White River Junction, the signs of the new landscape were beginning to show. The mountains, although old and weather worn, had new peaks, valleys had gotten deeper and were devoid of any vegetation. There were signs everywhere that a tsunami had made its way far inland. The Connecticut River had receded back to its original size after flooding the area completely and scraping the land along the

12A to a clean unadulterated flood plain. The entire town of West Lebanon was gone, and basements and footings were all that could be seen. As if by some divine intervention, the bridge over the river was intact, and this was the route that Steve and Jenna took. They were looking for a building that was still standing and would make a good homestead. As they drove down the North Plainfield Road, there was not much to see until Mt. Finish appeared on the horizon. A road that headed to the mountain was also the connector to the Lebanon Municipal Airport, the old Commerce Avenue that ran to the perimeter of the airport. The altitude was more than 600 feet above sea level, and they found a small farm located on the side of the mountain with a white two story semi-detached farmhouse. There was a two car garage adjacent to the house, and two big red barns up on the hill. The landscape was clear, but after months of neglect, very overgrown.

Steve and Jenn got out of the car and went to the front door. A weathered screen door met them. The screen had seen better days and Steve could not see through it. The windows were covered and there was no way to see what was inside the home.

"Should I knock?" said Steve.

"Of course you should knock, there might still be someone here. It doesn't look like there was any damage."

Steve knocked on the door. He waited for a minute or two and knocked again. No one came to the door. Steve then opened the screen door. It complained, as all screen doors do when being opened, and the grinding of the springs sent a chill down his spine. The white storm door was also weathered; paint was chipping off of it and the single window on the top had a piece of paper in it. Steve read the note to Jenn:

"If our home has survived, please feel free to come in and rest. The key is on a nail under the porch. We have gone to Maine to be with our family and God: we do not know if we will return. If we do not survive, we hope who ever finds our home will make it their own and make good use of the twenty-five acres of farmland that we have taken care of in our retirement.

There is a tractor in the biggest barn, and the smaller barn held our livestock of 5 cows, 10 pigs, and a dozen chickens. We let them roam free before we left.

We pray to God that we will all survive, and hope to meet the people who have taken over our home."

Richard and Maryann Steve.

Steve went under the porch and found the key. He brought it up to the door and unlocked the dead bold and latch. The door opened to a typical farm house. Stairs led up to the second floor on the right, the living room was to the left, and down the hall a there was a kitchen that took up the entire back of the house. It was in immaculate condition. The furniture was covered by heavy blankets and tarps to protect the material. There was a big painter's tarp on the floor, and when Jenna lifted it up, the wood floor underneath showed it was well cared for. They both walked into the kitchen and couldn't believe their eyes. Stainless steel appliances open and cleaned before Richard and Maryann left. There was no spoiled food in the refrigerator, no opened packages in the cupboards. It was as if they were planning on going on long trip and cleaned everything up for the return. Jenna was the first to speak.

"Oh my God Steve, can you believe this? Look at the condition of everything, clean, no garbage, no rodents, nothing. There's even food in the pantry. Freeze-dried, canned, and packaged. Water, flour, juice, even powered milk. I haven't seen this stuff in twenty years." Steve agreed, speechless, but he knew what he had to do.

"Ok, Jenna, gather up anything you can find to

show previous owners, and the note. We'll have to take it to the information center tomorrow to register our claim."

"But the note said they would be back, God willing. Should we make a claim to this property? Or should we just get it ready for their return and do as they ask and rest?"

"I think we have to stake a claim, Jenna," he said softly. "They left a note that stated they were going to Maine, and we both know that most of Maine is underwater now: the areas that weren't flooded were wiped clean by the tsunamis."

"All right. I hope they survived, but it would have been against the worst that nature could have thrown at them. Unless they were staying with their family in the Snow Mountain region, they couldn't have survived. I'll go see what I can find upstairs; you look in the pantry and the living room."

They both started to explore the house. Jenna found the Deed and the passports of Richard and Maryann. They were a couple in their mid fifties, and from the smiles on their faces, even in the passport photos, she could sense that they really had a zest for life. She also found an old-fashioned photo album and home movies and video of the property taken before they had to leave. As she watched the videos she started to cry. She felt for this couple who cared so deeply for each other and their lifestyle. She watched as they playfully gave a tour of the barns, old Bessie (their first electric tractor), and the generator station behind the back barn.

"Steve! Steve! Come here, quickly, you've got to see this." Steve heard Jenna's shattered voice. He did not know what was wrong, but the hair on his neck felt like it was standing straight out. He ran up the stairs, tripping on the last step in his haste to get to her. He ran down the hallway and entered the master bedroom to find her sitting on the bed, tears running down her face, and a big smile when he appeared at the door.

"They have a generator plant behind the last barn. They were living off the grid."

"No shit! Really?" Steve could not believe what he was seeing: the solar generator, wind turbine, storage batteries and converters, all in a concrete building. He watched as Richard explained that he was dismantling the system to protect it from any damage. Richard was giving a step-by-step lesson on how to hook everything back up when it was safe to do so. He mentioned that the batteries were fully charged, but would drain down over the course of time and would have to be recharged in a very specific way as to maintain their lifetime. He said that once the turbine was back up and the solar cells outside again, the batteries had to be hit with everything that could be generated for eight hours to refresh them. One that has been accomplished can the next day be used to put a small load on, like charging the tractor, and then on the third day the inverter can be turned on and the house will have power again.

Steve sat on the bed next to Jenna, slack-jawed. He could not believe their luck.

"Jenna, we're going to have to go into the information center this afternoon. We've stumbled on to something fantastic, and have to register right away."

Jenna agreed, and gathered up the papers. On their way down the stairs, Steve went to the front door again and removed the note, and took the key and put it in his pocket.

"Thanks, Richard," he said and then went to the kitchen.

"I'm going out to the barns first, Jenna; I've got to see for myself what is there and what kind of condition its in."

"Ok. I'll fix some lunch if you can bring in the coolers.

"Sure, I'll do that first." He went to the car and retrieved the coolers and their clothes, leaving everything on the back porch for Jenna to take into the house. He then walked to the biggest barn, opened the big bay door and there was Bessie the tractor, a big green electric John Deere with a full cab and a hay cutting system. On the other side of the barn was a plow blade, hay bailer, and a lawn mower. Steve chuckled. "I guess you and I are going to be close friends for the next little while."

In the next barn, Steve found livestock still living. Behind this barn the gate was open and the animals were scattered across the fields, but not far from the barn. When they saw Steve, they started back to the barn, obviously mistaking him for Richard. Steve didn't know what to do, and as the cows started to run, he panicked and ran through the barn and slammed the door closed. At that point, he started to laugh, as he put it all together. They weren't attacking him; they were coming to see him. He opened the door again, and was met by four very dirty cows and a half a dozen pigs. He couldn't call the pigs dirty; they just seemed normal. He assumed that because the barn had not been kept up in awhile the animals beds were a mess. The smell of cow and sheep manure then hit his nostrils full force, and it was refreshing.

He told the animals he'd be back, and closed the door. He went to the small concrete building in the back and opened the door with the combination code that Richard had left on the video. There were no windows and no lights: the illumination came from the open door. Steve inspected the entire building and the footings behind it for the wind turbines. There were two 20-foot masts, with bases for them and their guide wires. Richard also showed how to take the turbines down and put them back up with the tractor's winch. Everything was where he said it would be, and tomorrow would be a busy day.

Steve made his way back to the house and came into the back porch.

"Wipe your shoes off, mister!," yelled Jenna. She then burst into laughter that brought tears to her eyes. Steve joined in, and together they had a difficult time eating their lunch of prepared pasta and preserved fruit, giggling at almost every bite.

Over lunch Steve explained to Jenna how he now saw their plans.

"We'll we have to reevaluate things now. We were going to help the community by working with others; now I think we should become merchants and provide for the community.

Jenna nodded. "Yes, we have the means to provide for our community and should register as such when we get to the Information Center. I'll start requesting the proper seeds from the central repository, and we should be able to plant in the spring."

"Agreed. After all, I think it will take most of the winter to figure out the equipment."

"Oh, wait," said Jenn, "there isn't going to be a winter, remember? The briefing said the seasons are north and south, now that the earth is on an even axis. The season for growing is now all year round, and the weather here is going to be what we have today, mostly sunny and in the low 20s."

"I forgot that. I guess I'll have to learn faster then. But I'm sure the Information Center will help." They finished their lunch and packed up the papers for the five-minute drive back to the Information Center at White River Junction. Driving along the countryside, more and more people were starting to appear. Steve noticed the ragged look of most of them, but to see smiles on a few lightened his heart.

They drove down the main street and pulled into the parking lot of the White River Junction Information Center. Steve parked the car and Jenn got out. Steve instinctively went to the parking meter, and then realized that he didn't have any change and it wasn't needed anyway. The cashless society had begun.

In the Information Center, Steve and Jenn approached the property management counter. An elderly gentleman whose name tag read George Henderson greeted them.

"Hi folks, welcome to White River Junction. How can I help you?"

"Well George, I'd like to register a property and business with the department. We have located a small farm about five miles up the road and would like to stake a claim and set up the operation again."

"A small farm—boy, that will be great news for the folks around here, fresh produce is something we haven't seen in a very long time." George turned in his chair to type in the information on the papers Steve handed him. "Oh, I see you're at the Steve's farm. It sure was a pity to hear about Richard and Maryann."

"You knew the owners?" Steve asked.

"Yep, played cards with them both every Tuesday night."

Steve could hear the melancholy tone in George's voice. It sounded like these were two people he really admired.

"They went to Maine to help out his family; the last report said they died when the tsunamis wiped the coast clean. Most of the area is now under 50 or 60 meters of ocean. A real shame, but that was Richard, he would have done anything for anybody, and stood by and protected his family with every last breath he had."

George had finished entering all the information and printed out the acquisition forms for Steve and Jenna to sign, as well as the new identity badges for each. These badges signified that they were merchants, and could acquire items needed for their farm.

"Now you understand that once you're up and running, you'll have to bring me the first basket of vegetables." George said with a wink.

"Of course, of course," said Jenna, "but only if you come out to play cards every now and then."

"It's a deal. Now take these papers over to the probate window and you'll be on your way. The market opens every morning at 9:00, but as people start coming back, those hours may change. Back in the day a good cup of coffee and conversation, or gossip as the missus would say, started promptly at 6:00. You folks take care and call if you need anything."

Steve and Jenna went to the probate window, and were again greeted by someone wearing a name tag. Jillian Baker looked up from her computer screen, and with what could be described as absolute glee, reached out to shake their hands.

"Land sakes alive, more folks setting up shop. It's so wonderful to see y'all here. Welcome, welcome. I've been reviewing the file George sent over and you're all set to go. There is normally a waiting period of 30 days, but with the note from Richard and Maryann, we'll treat this as a transfer of title. Congratulations!" She put all the papers together and gave the big envelope to Jenna. "I do hope you get up and running soon, we'd love to see y'all come into town this Saturday night for the big party. There's gonna be music, dancing, speeches, and homemade food. I'm so excited; we haven't had a Saturday night like this in ages."

The jolly woman's enthusiasm was contagious. "We'll be there with bells and whistles on. What do you want us to bring?"

"Honey, just the shirts on your back. There is no need for you to bring anything now. Later on when you're settled you can help out any way you see fit."

Steve interrupted, tapping his watch out of Jillian's sight. "Well we should get back and start setting up."

Jenna saw his tapping motion and nodded. "We've got a lot of work ahead of us. We'll see you Saturday night; thank you for the invite."

Steve and Jenna made their way to the car, walking briskly and not looking back. When they closed the doors, they burst out in an uncontrollable fit of laughter.

"Oh my god, am I ever glad we've finally met some people who aren't depressed." Jenna couldn't speak; she motioned that she was going to wet her pants, but still could not get any words out, just high pitched squealing noises.

"Ok, I understand, that was a hoot. I can't wait until Saturday night." Jenna nodded in agreement, tears streaming down her face, and looking at Steve with great relief. "Right then, let's go to the market, pick up some supplies and head back." Steve caught himself; he just couldn't bring himself to call the Stevens' farm home yet. It may feel like home some day, but right now, he was going to resurrect the Stevens' dream farm with the help of Richard himself and the videos that he left behind.

Chapter 7

September 15, 2030. Raymond was getting his second coffee of the morning, going over the papers and draft bills for the assembly. His job was done, and now it was up to the leaders of each country to ratify the Global Communities Bill of Rights and start to rebuild the human civilization. The many reports he received were encouraging: people were setting up communities all over the world and so far things were working out. Manufacturing plants, farms, and shops were starting to open again. Community Information Centers were working out well and no real problems had been encountered.

Raymond's phone rang. "Good morning, Dr. Braemore here." Raymond's call display on his vidphone did not show who was calling.

"Dr. Braemore, this is Patrick Corpert's office. Please stand by for Mr. Corpert." Raymond was confused: normally Patrick would call himself. Why the formality?

"Raymond? Patrick here, thanks for waiting."

"Any time, Patrick. What's up?"

"Well, as you know the assembly is in a couple of hours, my office has had a chance to go over the drafts you submitted and I must be honest, this is amazing stuff. I'm sure that we will get these resolutions passed with no problem. I want to ask you something." Raymond knew that there was something coming, something big, yet somewhat expected.

"The GC emergency council had a meeting yesterday and voted for you to be the first Chancellor of the GC—that is, if you want the job. As your draft states, it will be a 10-year position, but since you have had your hand on the pulse of the world for the past year, it is only fitting that you are the man to lead us."

Raymond took a long breath. He could take the position and see the changes through to the very end: did he have it in himself to last 10 years while mankind found its way?

"Patrick, I'm honored that the council has seen fit to bestow this honor on me, and to be frank I'll accept it under two conditions."

"Two conditions? What might they be, Raymond?"

"First, I get to pick my staff. You already know

most of them, and we work well together. Second, I want an early exit clause. I need to be able to judge when we have passed the milestones and can self-govern again. I'll then call an election at that time."

"Ok, Raymond. Those are reasonable requests. Let me call around and I'll let you know before the assembly. Oh, and Raymond, please be about fifteen minutes late so I can get a vote and approval on this. It's going to be a piece of cake, but it would be best if you weren't there until it has been formalized."

"No problem, Patrick. I guess I'll have to write an acceptance speech now. Good thing I have a couple of hours and a fresh pot of coffee."

Patrick laughed. "Yes, a fresh pot of coffee can make miracles happen. See you soon, Raymond."

Raymond hung up the phone, sat down at his table and looked outside. He marveled at the scenery. From his modest apartment suite on top of the Command and Control Center in Salt Lake City, he could see the mountains to the east, now devoid of snow caps, and to the south, the new ring on the horizon. The sky was a deep blue, and not a cloud in the sky. Raymond figured it would be a few months before clouds began to return. After Gaia, the atmosphere was scrubbed of humidity and impurities, natural evaporation was taking place, but the effect was called "ground heating" by meteorologists. The ground would heat up in the day, and rain in the evening would restore the balance again.

Raymond finished his coffee and went to his bedroom to get ready for the assembly. He walked into his bed room and to the closet. He picked out his best navy blue suit, a pressed white shirt from a hanger and a royal blue tie. He made sure nothing was out of place as he dressed; he combed his graying hair, and took one more look in the full length mirror.

"Ok, Mr. Chancellor, you're ready." He went to the kitchen, put his papers in his black briefcase and picked up the phone to call for his driver.

"Hi Tim, I'll be in front of the C&C in 10 minutes. Yes, heading to the assembly. See you then." He closed his suite door and walked to the elevator. Jocelyn was also coming down the hallway: Tim had called her the moment Raymond hung up the phone.

"Good morning, Jocelyn."

"Good morning Dr. Braemore. You look very nice this morning." Raymond, not accustomed to getting compliments, blushed and nodded.

"We have a very eventful day ahead of us. I think history is about to be written." Jocelyn remarked. "I have your opening speech finalized from your draft, and the draft of the Rights Bill and the recovery plan have been placed on the secure data link, time stamped for opening when you start your presentation. Your arrival is scheduled for 10:15 at the assembly and I've notified Simon, Roy, Sebastian and Gena to be at the assembly at 11:15."

"Very good. I don't know how I'd function without you, Jocelyn."

"Just doing my job, and loving it." She smiled.

Raymond and Jocelyn exited the elevator and walked through the secure hallway to the black limousine that was waiting for them. Tim opened the door to the back and made sure everyone was inside and belted in before signaling to the escort vehicles they were ready for the 10 minute ride to the assembly.

In the limo things were very quiet. Raymond was reading the status reports from China, Russia and Africa. No major problems; Africa was having a hard time getting fresh water, but the desalinization plants in Egypt were coming back online, and the solar plants in the Congo and Brazil were not able to get enough sunlight to generate at full capacity.

Raymond made a note to have these relocated further south to take advantage of the unobstructed sunlight. It was apparent the opaque ring around the earth was blocking about fifty percent of the sunlight at the equator.

Raymond also noticed that the Sahara Desert was experiencing regular rain fall. Unexpected, but beneficial, since there is a lot of land to be reclaimed in Africa, he thought. The reports outlined the migration back to the surviving towns and cities. Most of the manufacturing had come back online, and harvesting of food was planned for the upcoming months.

One observation Raymond made through all of the reports was the community-based markets. The Information Centers reported the establishment of local markets, thriving businesses selling locally made products, and each community had pulled together to establish self-sufficiency. He read about the White River Junction community in the North American briefing, located along the Vermont and New Hampshire border, the population growing to 300,000 citizens, and the growth of the information center. A local government had been put in place; police, emergency, even health services were up and running, and very successful. The community also applied for accreditation for the new health sciences university.

How odd that a little community like White River Junction would become the shining example of the new order in a very short time. The citizens there were pulling together to build on what they already knew. The Information Center also submitted the numbers of new Identity Cards issued, and White River Junction had the most new issues to non-registered evacuees. It looked like fifty percent of the population came from areas that did not evacuate.

The limousine arrived at the assembly promptly at 10:05, giving Raymond ten minutes to prepare. Jocelyn and Raymond walked into the waiting room, and opened their video tablets. Raymond opened up his documents, entered the password, and released the documents to the delegate's tablets. The timing sequence was set to sync with his tablet so no one could read ahead.

From the assembly floor, applause erupted and cheers for Raymond could be heard. Jocelyn looked at Raymond, went over to him to straighten his tie, and like a mother sending her child out on stage for the first time, said, "It's your time, break a leg. Show them what you can do."

"Thanks. Let's get it started." Raymond winked at Jocelyn and walked to the assembly stage. The assembly's delegates rose in thunderous applause. Raymond held his head high and waved: he noticed Simon, Roy, Gena and Sebastian in the front row, beaming with excitement. He looked back to see Jocelyn standing in the wings, tears streaming down her face. He stepped up to the podium, shook Secretary Corpert's hand and waited for the applause to stop.

"Esteemed guests of the first assembly of the Global Community, I welcome you to Utah, and I accept the position you have bestowed upon me. It is with a heavy heart and immense gratitude that I will strive to perform this task to the best of my ability." The applause erupted again, and as it died down, Raymond put his head down and spoke softly into his lapel microphone. "Can we please have a minute's silence to remember those who perished, our loved ones, friends and families, for the crews who did all they could to evacuate as many people as possible, for the unsung heroes of the Information Centers, and those who gave their lives to protect mankind's existence."

The assembly became very quiet. Some sobs could be heard and whispered prayers. Raymond looked up after about 45 seconds to see no faces. Everyone was looking at the ground and in silent remembrance. He let the silence continue for another two minutes, then slowly brought up the video screens behind him and the delegate's tablets.

"Thank you. What you see before you is the final Global Community Bill of Rights. I'm glad to see that there have been no revisions from our original draft: it makes implementation easier. I would also like to acknowledge the team that put this together; you'll get to meet them in a few minutes."

"First I would like to make the following motion. We the Assembly of the Global Community hereby adopt the document titled "Global Community Bill of Rights" to be the first document that makes up the base of the Global Community Charter. And be it also moved that each representative present in this assembly be the dually appointed representative of the Chancellor of the Global Community, who will be responsible for ensuring that the citizens are informed and adhere to the Global Community Bill of Rights."

Secretary Corpert immediately seconded the motion and called for the vote. Within a minute the first resolution of the new Global Community had been passed and was now official. The next chapter in mankind's history had begun.

Applause filled the assembly; after a few minutes Raymond put up his hand.

"Ok, now to get down to the business of doing business." Raymond adjusted his glasses and motioned for a chair. This was going to take some time, but the details were important and had to be clearly understood.

"The first order of business is to introduce the team who will help you. I would like Simon Gross, Roy Davis, Gena Regas, Sebastian Gore and Patrick Corpert to stand."

Secretary Corpert was shocked when he heard his name. He thought that he would not be involved in the new governing body, and when chosen, he was humbled, but stood any way.

"These five people will make up my cabinet of advisors; each will be responsible for directing your departments, and assisting with decisions.

Patrick Corpert will be the director of Global Community Security and be the top official of the military and police forces globally. I want to stress that these are peace keepers, and rights enforcement officers.

Simon Gross will be the Director of Economics.

He will lead the Identity Card and transaction teams to ensure that no one is left out and no one is abusing the system.

Gena Regas will be the Director of Education and Manufacturing. She'll help the transition teams retool what is necessary for manufacturing and set up the education system.

Sebastian Gore will be the Director of the Environment. His duties include the research into alternative fuels and methods to preserve the environment, as well overseeing the monitoring of global recycling and emissions.

Ray Davies will be the Director of Transitions and Exploration, leading teams to enhance our methods and to continue on with the space program.

Finally, Jocelyn Burris-Stone will be my executive director and Vice Chancellor. Jocelyn has been instrumental in making sure I have all my facts together and knows as much as I do with regards to our grand plan.

Esteemed delegates, I give to you the first Global Community Caucus."

Applause again erupted in the assembly. Raymond then spent the next few hours outlining the specific duties each of his team, as well as taking questions from the floor. The ideas were flowing and everything was coming together. Time would tell how successful this exercise would be.

After the formalities, delegates from all the corners of the earth were divided into working groups, with each Director to lay out the plans and explain how to report progress. The first priority was Identity Cards for all; the second priority was to get the manufacturing engines rolling again and the movement of goods and services that would be required by the citizens. Priorities were set for Health, Education, Manufacturing, Resources and of course Social Programs.

For Raymond his delegated positions were working well, and he felt comfortable with the progress. It was now time to visit the Command and Control Center and arrange for a global tour to see firsthand the damage and meet with the citizens. Raymond was going to be very visible during his tenure, and ensure that everyone felt equal to each other.

In the Command and Control Centre, things were considerably quieter than the last time Raymond was here. He knocked on Stuart's door.

"Hey, how is my good friend Atlas holding up?"

Stuart laughed and put his hands over his head. "The world doesn't seem so heavy these days."

"Good to hear, Stuart. And how is she holding up?"

"The good news, Raymond, is that the climates have settled, and the humidity in the upper atmosphere is starting to rise. Snow is falling in the Arctic and Antarctic regions, and ice is starting to form. We have indications that the Gulf Stream is flowing again, so everyone that thought it was driven by temperatures is wrong. It is run by the spinning of the earth and I think it will help jump start the climate system. The North Pacific Drift is also running again and dissipating some of the heat from the ring of fire volcanoes, and it looks like the Hawaiian Islands have returned. I'd love to fly over there and see what new islands look like. I don't think they will be ready for humans for some time though."

Raymond was hanging on every word. He and Stuart predicted the outcome and it looked like they had been very accurate. Stuart had charts, maps, and oceanographic data at his finger tips and loved every minute of it.

"Stuart, how would you like to head up the Meteorological and Geophysical department of the Global Community?"

"I'd be interested. What do you need me to do?"

"Well, I'm not sure of the setup required, but you'll have establish the monitoring of weather and geological events, forecasting, and tracking the seasonal changes along the latitudinal grids."

"Sounds easy enough." Stuart raised his eyebrows. "Of course, any historical data we have is useless now so I guess I'll have to start from scratch."

"Whatever you need, Stuart; while you're setting up shop, also consider training for new meteorologists and geologists. We'll need them soon as well."

Stuart plopped down in his chair, feigning a look of desperation. "Thanks for the good news, Ray, and for letting me take things easy." Raymond laughed.

"Any time, old friend." He turned and walked out of Stuart's office, over to the C&C general's console.

"General, I would like for you to pass on to your staff and peers that I think you did a fantastic job. I'm proud of the job you folks did helping to save so many lives. When we get a chance to take a breather, we'll have one hell of a party."

General Simkinson saluted Raymond. "Thank you, Sir. A pleasure to serve. I can't wait for the party: I hope it's sooner rather than later."

"You can count on that. I'll advise you in the next week of the date. As you were."

"Yes Sir." General Simkinson returned to his console and flashed a thumbs up to his staff.

Raymond continued out the C&C and went to the elevator for the lift to his suite. Jocelyn appeared just as the doors to the elevator were closing.

"Hold the door!" She called. When the door opened again, Raymond was looking at her with some amusement. He had never heard Jocelyn raise her voice; he found it refreshing.

"Come on in, Vice Chancellor. And how are you now?"

"To tell you the truth Dr. Braemore, rather overwhelmed."

"Well, first things first, you can call me Ray; and secondly, you deserve it. No one knows how much you have put into this better than me. I think you're going to do just fine. For your first order of business, you need to find two executive assistants: one for me and one for you."

Having been an executive assistant all of her professional career, Jocelyn felt strange to suddenly have an assistant of her own. To give up control of Raymond's day-to-day schedule was going to be hard, even harder than the new job itself.

The elevator stopped at the executive suites, and

Raymond and Jocelyn headed to their suites. Ray stopped before entering his door.

"Jocelyn, I think we have to find new living quarters as well. Have our new assistants locate two houses fairly close to the Global Community Assembly, and arrange security details for both."

"Ok, Dr. Brea...I mean Ray. Do you want a two-storey or single-storey home?"

"Two-storey with a study would work just fine, thanks." Raymond entered his suite, but before the door closed he turned. "Oh, and please make sure they have a view of the mountains."

"Ok Ray, two-storey with a study and a view, got it." Raymond's door closed. He walked into his bedroom and took off his suit and started the shower. As the water came up to temperature he went to his closet and found an old FDNY sweatshirt and a pair of blue jeans. This was going to be a relaxing evening with nothing on his plate. He then picked up the phone.

"Chef Voutour? Raymond Braemore."

"Yes Dr. Breamore, I recognized the number. How can I help you?"

"I would like something for supper, and I want you to surprise me with one of your creations. I'll also need a wine, and a dessert."

"Certainly. I have just the dish in mind, we did some baking this morning and a fresh load of produce came in from the valley. I'm sure there is some lamb in the refrigerators so I'll create something you'll enjoy. Is this for one or two?"

Raymond thought for a moment: it had been so long since he had a meal with someone in a social setting that he almost forgot. "Hang on one second, Chef." Raymond punched the hold button, and then picked another line. "Hi, it's me. Have you had supper yet? No? Great, meet me here in an hour." He picked the first line. "It's going to be two, Chef, thanks."

Raymond put the phone down, and walked towards the shower, thinking to himself *this is going to be good*. He removed his underwear and stepped into the flowing water, adjusted the pressure and let the massaging streams of water run across his neck and back. As the warmth surrounded his body, he turned around and sat on the stool, directly under the water. His eyes closed and he let the events of the day replay one more time. A University professor, dedicating his life to teaching students on how to make a better world, now has the power and position to practice what he had been preaching. How ironic that he would get the job, how ironic that his life turned out the way it did.

The water continued to wash away the tension and turmoil of the day. Raymond let his mind clear, the sound of the water acting like white noise: his mind was now devoid of any thoughts and it was a wondrous feeling.

Chef Voutour was busy in his kitchen. Since providing Raymond and Jocelyn with a great lunch that fateful day some months ago, he was promoted to the executive chef of the Global Community Assembly. He was going over the shipment of produce that arrived: fresh zucchini, radishes, romaine lettuce, beefeater tomatoes, green, red and yellow peppers. Idaho potatoes, spaghetti squash, and strawberries. He checked the produce and was very impressed with the quality. Then he went to the walk in refrigerator and found a rack of lamb that came in yesterday from Sheep Lane off of the 133 near Stansbury Park.

The menu was complete for Dr. Breamore. Roasted rack of lamb with roasted potatoes, a medley of zucchini, peppers and tomatoes, a fresh salad with a honey and vinegar dressing, and for dessert strawberry short cake.

"A feast fit for a king!" Chef Voutour said aloud, and most of his kitchen staff looked at him, startled by the sudden outburst.

"Sorry, folks, I'm excited about a meal I have to prepare personally. Who wants to help me prepare my *mise en place*?"

Every hand in the kitchen of thirty went up. The staff enjoyed working with Chef Voutour. His humble demeanor and instructional techniques made every day a learning experience for most of the young cooks. It was not every day the Chef actually cooked a meal, and to work with him was a great honor. Susan Spicer was the first to run up to Chef Voutour, and almost knocked him down.

"I can help, Chef" Her enthusiasm and skill made this an easy choice. "Ok, you can help, but I'll be watching you closely. If the potatoes are not perfect then…We'll do them again. Let's get to work. Here's the menu."

Chapter 8

Steve and Jenna were enjoying their farm life. It took Steve a little longer than he figured to set up the power system, but he did it. The evening he finished, there was enough power to light the house and the walkway lights. He let out a yelp of excitement; Jenna chirped in too from the kitchen window. She could finally use the stove and make a cup of tea. As she turned on the burner the lights faded and then went out.

"Ok, what did you do?" She called out to Steve.

"Nothing, hang on." Steve checked the wiring again, went over the diagram Richard had drawn and could not find anything wrong. He started to talk to himself. "Red to red, yep, red to red; then green to green, and there it is, green to green. Yellow to the battery bank 1, yep. White to battery bank 2, yep. Green and yellow to battery bank 3, but do not connect for 24 hours. Ah, there's what you did

Steve, dumbass, you connected the wires before it was time."

Jenn could hear the mumbling from the power house. "Who are you talking to, Steve?"

"No one, Honey. Just some dumbass who can't follow directions to the letter. I found the problem; just give me five more minutes."

"Ok. When it's running do you want a cup of tea?"

"Yes. I'll even go to the barn to get some milk."

Steve disconnected the green and yellow wires, started the generator and released the windmill brakes. The hum of power being generated filled the room. He checked the gauges and the amperage was fine, the volts were within limits and the batteries were now charging. Steve pushed up the big switch to the house and this time everything was energized. The house was on 110V power and working.

Steve turned off the lights and headed to the main barn. He and Jenna managed to find four of the five cows wandering around the property. They also found 24 chickens and 15 pigs. More than what was left behind. They both had a laugh over the numbers, joking about one pig saying to the other, "come on...It's the end of the world...one more time for old time's sake." And the chickens, "the sky is falling...what the hell, we might as well make the rooster happy one more time."

Needless to say the farm was off and running very quickly. Steve repaired the back of the barn, and Jenna helped by cleaning out the old hay and straw replacing it with fresh clippings from the two fields Steve harvested shortly after he got the tractor running.

Steve went into the brightly lit barn to milk one of the cows; he learned how to do this through much trial and error. The cow he practiced on didn't like him very much, but he figured she'd get over it. In the barn he gathered the stool and milking bucket and went to the first stall. Just before he entered he saw a switch and another note.

This switch controls the milking machine. It has been stored in the loft and can do three cows at a time. The plug receptacle is in the back of stall 2. Make sure the stalls are locked before you turn it on. Instructions and a video are also in the milking machine's crate.

Steve started to laugh. Is seemed Richard Steves really enjoyed his farm, and the gadgets to make it easier to run. He sat beside a cud-chewing Holstien cow, and proceeded to milk a gallon of fresh milk from her. When he was finished, he put the stool away and poured the milk in to a clean gallon container. He washed and sterilized the milking bucket, then hung it up to dry. He thought to himself how funny it was that Richard's meticulous methods had rubbed off on him. Everything was clean and put back in its place. Steve learned how to do things on the farm from one of the best teachers: the fact that he was no longer alive did not seem to matter. To Steve the hours of video instruction were as if Richard was videoconferencing to him. Richard even had a habit of pausing for questions, even though he couldn't hear them.

Steve made his way through the back porch, took off his boots at the door and came inside to the kitchen. He gave Jenna a kiss and put the gallon of milk on the counter. He then went to the refrigerator and started it the way he was shown by another one of Richard's videos.

"There, we should be able to refrigerate things in a couple of hours."

Jenna looked at him from the stove. "You've become quite the handy man, haven't you?"

"I had the best teacher in the world," Steve said, moving over to the basement door. I'm going to turn on the hot water storage unit now, and in the morning no more cold showers!"

Jenna giggled. "Oh no. If you can't take any more cold showers, that means—well, um, we might have to work on that."

Steve and Jenna were growing closer each day, but with the amount of work to do around the farm, both were exhausted by nightfall. They had started to share a bed a couple of days after they moved in, but nothing further, and mostly out of the necessity to stay warm. They did not have time to think about the next level in their relationship until now, and they both wanted to make this their home. They talked many nights of getting married and starting a family, but talk was all they could muster. As the farm started to take shape, more time was freed up to talk more, and enjoy each other's company—nights on the porch listening to the returning wildlife, or sitting in the living room reading and talking about their days were becoming more common place. During the last evening's rain shower, a thunderstorm made its way around the mountains and Jenna, a little scared, had cuddled up with Steve to watch the light show.

They sat down at the kitchen table. It was late evening and the lights were on: no more candles.

"Well, I think we took a major step today." Steve started. "We now have power, hot water, a milking machine, and tomorrow I think we should go get some seeds and start to plant the north field."

"What should we plant? My fingers aren't green, not even my thumb," Jenna said. "I tried to grow a small flower garden in New York, but it didn't survive.

"I wouldn't worry about that. I think if we plant grain, then we can make breads, and the south field should be ready for harvest for the cows and pigs."

Jenn nodded. "Oh, yeah, the pigs. What are we going to do with them?"

"Well, two of the sows are pregnant, so I think we have to take three or four to the market. I can slaughter them, but as for cutting specific chops from them, I have no idea. Hopefully someone at the market can butcher them for us." Steve felt uneasy about killing anything, but also realized that he was a farmer now, and this had to be done. The pigs would be fairly easy, but the cows were a different story. They were too big and still producing milk.

Jenna thought about it for a moment. "You know, we did meet that other farmer at the market the other day. I think we should talk to him to see if he can help."

"Sure. Any direction or help would be appreciated. I think we can give him a pig for himself and a side of beef when we are ready for the cows."

"Ok, mister farmer, enough talk about killing animals. I think we should head to bed. Maybe you should take a shower." There was a twinkle in her eye and a jump in her step. Steve didn't even let his teacup stop rocking; he was on his way upstairs.

The next morning, Steve and Jenna were cuddled in bed when the sun came up.

"Good morning," she whispered.

"Good morning," Steve said with a big smile. "You wouldn't happen to know where my best friend Jenna went, would you? I mean she was here last night, and then I dreamt that she turned into this goddess and made love to me. I was lost. I'm so madly in love with her I have to tell her."

Jenna stared at Steve. "Go on. Goddess, hmm? You mean this one?" She then rolled on top of Steve and started to kiss his chest.

"Yes that's her. That's…Oh hell, no more talk."

Jenna and Steve both lay on the bed staring up at the ceiling, smiling and feeling complete. After a few minutes Steve rolled on to his side to look at her: her hair was mussed and small beads of sweat were still visible on her lip. He kissed her, but pulled back before she could respond in kind.

"I think we should stop at the Information Center after the market, don't you?"

"What for?"

"Well, if I'm going to be sharing a bed and a home, I want to share it with my wife and best friend."

Jenna smiled. "Oh you mean to get married? I'm not sure…I might be spoken for?"

Steve enjoyed her teasing, but now was not the time. "Jenn I'm trying to be serious, I think we should get married."

"So do I, Steve. I agree, let's do it today."

"Ok." Steve got out of bed and in all his naked glory got down on one knee, grabbed Jenna's hand, looked her in the eyes and said, "Jenna Vierra, will you be Mrs. Stephen Bower?"

Tears came to her eyes. After the last few years of turmoil, heartbreak and loss, she finally had a perfect moment to say "Yes."

He kissed her and gave her a very strong hug. "I'll always protect and cherish you."

Once they got moving, Steve showered and Jenna made her way down to the kitchen. The fresh aroma of coffee filled the house, succeeded by that of pancakes and toast. Steve came downstairs wearing one of Richard's suits. Jenna almost choked on her coffee: it was a double-breasted, red tartan affair, with white shoes.

"Ok, Richard might have been a genius and a fantastic engineer, but his sense of style was lacking."

"You are so right. Please tell me you're not wearing this to town?"

"Oh, ok, if you insist." Steve said while doing a couple of poses.

"I do." Jen stood with her arms crossed.

"Remember those words. I'll go change." Steve ran back up stairs, laughing as he put on his best pair of jeans and cleanest golf shirt. He though a moment about keeping the white shoes on, but decided sneakers would do, considering Jenna would probably kill him and murder was no way to start a marriage.

Jenna met Steve on the stairs. "My turn for a shower and to get changed, but I promise, nothing as gaudy as that suit."

"Is the coffee is still on?"

"Yes. See you in a few minutes."

Steve went to the barn to do the morning chores, being very careful not to get dirty. He collected the eggs, fed the cows and pigs, and made mental notes to hook up the milking machine and enquire at the market how to make cheese.

He loaded the truck and unplugged it from the

generating station. This reminded him to go back into the power house and hook up the green and yellow wire to battery bank 3. When he opened the door and turned on the light, all the gauges were showing green. He hooked up the wire and the solar array was now online, storing power. He checked the gauges and saw that they were generating a lot of power. An idea struck him—this could be used as a bartering tool. He kept that thought and closed things up. Jenna emerged from the house with two travel mugs of coffee; they got into the truck and made their way to the morning market.

The White River Junction market had grown over the past few months to a two-acre site. Merchants had set up shops with a wide variety of goods and products. There were clothing shops that provided new products obtained from the evacuation center stores, and farmers set up their booths with their products ranging from produce, fruits and meats. The community had become self-sufficient, growing and marketing all its items sourced from the area. Steve and Jenna went to their designated shop and started to unload their truck. Once Steve had the eggs unloaded, he went to the counter and turned on the Identity Card reader and computers. Jenna went about her task of setting up the shelves and unpacking some of the canned goods they had ordered through the central stores: their shop would not be a fully functional market until they started to harvest crops, but Jenna was working to set things up now in preparation for that day. she also started to interview some of the local teens for positions at the market. These people would be running the shop on a day-to-day basis so that she and Steve could concentrate on getting products to market.

Steve saw that the butcher next door was open and called to Jenna from the back door.

"I'm going over to talk to Barry about the pigs, Jenna." Jenna acknowledged Steve with a wave and carried on with the stocking.

Across from Steve and Jenn's market was Barry Simpson's market. Barry raised beef, chicken and feed grain. His market was one of the first to get refrigeration, and he took full advantage of it. The freezers were stockpiled with his meats and in front of his store fifty pound reusable bags of feed were piled high, creating a hallway effect leading to the meat counter.

"Hi, Barry." Steve called as he walked into the back of the market.

"Steve! Good to see you," came the reply, but

Steve could not see where it was coming from. "Over here, near the corn feed."

Barry Simpson was a tall man with broad shoulders and huge hands. He spent all of his life raising cattle in Virginia. When he evacuated to Utah with his family, he spent most of his time taking care of the animals that had been evacuated. He helped feed and keep them healthy, butchered only the ones that were needed and selected the prime stock needed for breeding. He proved his abilities many times, and was eventually put in charge of the livestock retention program. To ensure the different species survived and the gene pool remained viable, it was his duty to sort the prime animals for breeding from the ones that would be sent to slaughter.

When the evacuation order was lifted, Barry and his family heard that a lot of people were going to White River Junction to settle. He knew of the area and arrived a few weeks after Steve and Jenna. He acquired the Hartland Golf Course and set up his farming area there. The golf course's lush fairways, manicured roughs and greens were overgrown, but with high-quality Kentucky bluegrass, a preferred feed of his handpicked livestock. He then cultivated the driving ranges and surrounding areas for corn and oats for feed. After two months of back breaking work, he was ready to receive the 300 head of cattle and the 200 chickens he'd ordered. This was the number it was believed would sustain the population of White River Junction indefinitely. Barry used the formula of three servings of beef or chicken per person each week. The population forecast for the White River Junction was three hundred thousand, and the 300 head of cattle and their offspring should be sufficient. His corn and oat fields would provide enough feed for his herd and flock, and leave some extra to take to market.

Steve found Barry sitting on a fifty pound bag of corn, drinking coffee next to an old pot-bellied stove.

"Nice touch." Steve said pointing to the stove.

"It's something I saw in a picture from my grandfather's day. It seems people would go into town just to sit around the stove and tell stories. I like stories, and thought that this would be ideal. Mind you, I can't have a fire in the stove, but I don't think we need it for the warmth."

"I think you're right there." Steve sat on another bag of corn. "I think we need corn cob pipes, straw hats, and red undershirts." Barry let out a grunt of agreement.

"I was wondering if I can talk to you about a thought I had, Barry."

"Sure, Steve, anything. What's on your mind?"

"Well," Steve adjusted his sitting position, "I have some pigs that are going to have piglets soon, and that is going to upset the balance of my little farm. Jenna and I were wondering if we could partner up? I would supply the pigs for slaughter, you get to market the meat, and we could each keep a slaughtered pig for ourselves. Then we could also share some field area to grow feed corn for you."

Barry looked at Steve, nodded, and said "that sounds like a good deal. Done." He reached out his huge hand and shook Steve's. Barry did not need to talk a lot:, he loved working with the animals, and keeping company with good people. He liked Steve and Jenna, and was impressed at how far they had come with the farm. He considered himself a professional farmer, and to see two novices like Steve and Jenna get their homestead up and running in a couple of months impressed him. They met many times at the market, and Steve even told Jenna he had met Barry in Utah at the Information Center there one day—in fact, it might have been the day he first considered heading east.

Barry stood up. "You'll need a way to get your

pigs over to my slaughter house. Just call me and I'll send one of my boys over with the animal transport truck. Try to call about 24 hours before you want to send them over, then don't feed them anymore. The short trip will traumatize them and if they've eaten, my truck is going to get very messy. My boys like to help out, drive the trucks and farm equipment, but they are very squeamish when it comes to cleaning up after the animals. I blame that on their mother, sending them to school all the time." Barry winked at Steve and started to laugh.

"Great, that will work out fine for us," Steve said. "If you don't mind me asking, how is your power situation?"

"Fairly stable. We've had some dark nights due to the refrigeration units taking priority on our system, but not too bad."

"Well, I think I can help you out there. You're connected to the power grid, right?"

"Yep, and using about 40% off of the grid, but they haven't got the systems up to full capacity yet. The Information Center says some time next year they should be generating about 80 percent."

"Well, I'm producing surplus right now, and from the capacity of my system, I can easily send some your way to help out."

"That would be much appreciated, Steve—but how you would do it? Our farms are about three miles apart as the crow flies."

Steve started to grin. "It will be easy. I'm off the grid, but can turn a switch that will put my excess power into it. Then I tell the Power Utility Board that whatever I send to the grid gets routed to your farm. It is not the actual power I generate that gets to you, but if I put in 20 Kilowatt hours, then you get to increase your consumption by 20 Kilowatt hours. That should be enough to run your house and your disinfecting equipment in the slaughter house."

"Wow, you can do that? I'm impressed." A big smile came across Barry's face. Steve knew what was next—there would be a big joke at his expense—but that was ok with him.

"And to think that I thought you were a simple city boy who got thrown in to a pile of manure and told to make something out of it."

"Nope, I'm not that smart. I just had one of the best teachers in the world." Steve spent the next hour telling Barry about the videos that were left behind, and how Richard Steve showed him everything in great detail. As soon as Steve had finished talking about the power system, Jenna came through the back door.

"Hi boys, am I interrupting?"

"Not at all, Jenna." Barry stood up and removed his cap.

"Oh, sit down, I'm no one special."

Steve objected. "Ah, excuse me, I think today you're someone very special."

Barry's expression changed to confusion. "Why just today Steve? Why not everyday?"

"Good point Barry, and yes every day. But today, I think Jenna will agree, is a little more special."

Barry was a very smart man but a slow thinker. It always took a moment for him to absorb and process information and he liked it that way. Years ago he used to play jokes on his friends by not saying much about the conversations he was in, up to a point; then he would detail the pros and cons of a situation, or come up with new theories that even Einstein would be proud of. He did after all have a PhD in Philosophy from Virginia State University.

He paused for a couple of moments, then a big smile came across his face. He turned to Jenna. "You're going to have a baby?"

Jenna laughed. "Close. I'm going to have a husband. Very similar, I think."

Barry and Steve laughed, but Barry turned the tables on Steve, "Yep, I think you're right there, you still have to feed them, put clean clothes on their backs, and keep them out of trouble. Congratulations, you two, I wish you all the best. I can't wait to tell the wife—we'll have a reception for you. Let me talk to Karen and I'll call you two tonight around 6:00 to let you know when we can have it."

Jenna grabbed Steve's hand, pulling him towards the front door. Steve tried to let go, but in the end figured he better not show Barry a sign of weakness by not following a good woman. He called back to Barry:

"Thanks for everything! We'll talk tonight. I'm off to get hitched!"

At the Information Center, Steve and Jenna approached the Legal Document and Registration office. Before they opened the door, they squeezed each other's hands, and took deep breaths. Steve nodded and mouthed 1, 2, 3 and they both knocked on the door.

Louise Mercer looked up from her computer screen. "Come in."

Her office was sparse, hardly any paper around for a legal office. Louise prided herself on the fact she had a truly paperless office. No one she knew could make that claim; and as far as she could remember, no one has ever come close to the paperless office. In front of her big oak desk were two green leather arm chairs. Beside each was a computer terminal and tablet, each one tied into her main system. Steve and Jenna entered the office.

"Welcome. I'm Louise Mercer, Legal Attaché to the Global Community White River Plains Information Center. How can I help you?"

Steve tried to talk, but couldn't. Jenn squeezed his hand, looked at him and then back at Louise. "We would like to get married." Steve nodded.

"You've come to the right place. Have a seat. I'll have you both take a terminal and fill in your information; you can do most of by swiping your Identity Card. Then take great care to read all of the clauses and conditions." Louise was almost cold in her instructions, but it was more repetition than really feeling that way towards the process. Once the paperwork was completed, she warmed up to a very nervous Steve and a calm Jenna.

"Ok, that nasty part is over, now I have two questions. Do you, Stephen Bowing, take Jenna Vierra to be your lawful partner and wife?"

"I do." Steve said with no nervousness in his voice. He did want Jenna as his partner.

"And you, Jenna Vierra, do you take Stephen Bowing to be your lawful partner and husband?"

Without hesitation, Jenna said "I do."

"There. That was easy. You may now kiss the bride."

Jenn and Steve stood, embraced and kissed. When they turned around to look at Louise again, she was looking up at them and crying.

"I love weddings," she sobbed. "They're not like the old days, but still every time I see a couple really in love, I get teary. If you both would sign the video screen, I'll print out your marriage certificate. Oh, are you both keeping your last names, or how would you like to be known?"

Jenna answered that question. "I would like to be Mrs. Jenna Bowing."

"Alrighty then. Congratulations again, you two. It is now official." Louise handed Jenna and Steve an envelope with their marriage certificate in it.

"Your Identity Cards have been updated; you can now acquire items without a permit for children and babies. It might be premature, but you never know. Also, there is a onetime annual exemption for the acquisition of food items. This is so you can celebrate with friends and family, and Steve for you;

you'll never forget your anniversary and can acquire the necessary items for that time every year.

Again, congratulations, folks, you're the first couple to marry here since the evacuations. I wish you all the luck in the world."

Mr. and Mrs. Bower left the office hand in hand and headed to the truck for the short ride home.

Jenna couldn't contain her emotions on the trip home; she was bouncing up and down in the seat saying over and over, "Mrs. Bowing, Mrs. Bowing. I'm Mrs. Bowing."

Steve just smiled. After the past year of turmoil, things were now feeling right, and working out just fine. He pulled the truck into the driveway and slowed.

"There it is, Jenna, our home."

Steve finally called the farm home. He still felt guilty: after all, Richard and Maryann had made this place their home. For two strangers to move in and start calling it home didn't seem right. But now, after all of the videos from Richard, the care and the details, Steve finally felt that Richard and Maryann would be proud to have their home change hands.

He got out of the truck and ran around to the side, opening the door for Jenn, then put his arms around her and picked her up. He walked up the back stairs on to the porch. Jenn opened the door from Steve's arms, and they crossed the threshold to their home. He gave her a kiss and put her down. He then ran back to the porch and took off his boots.

Chapter 9

Jocelyn walked to her door and opened it, turned the lights off and stepped in to the hallway. She had butterflies in her stomach as she approached the elevator. She paused for a moment, and kept on moving down the hallway. She approached suite 801, took a deep breath and rang the doorbell. The door opened.

"Hi, you," said Raymond. "I'm glad you could make it."

"Well, I really didn't have too much to do tonight: get a couple of new assistants, find a couple of houses, and arrange staffing. Minor stuff that can wait until tomorrow."

"I agree. In fact, I have a new request for you."

Jocelyn, not having brought her tablet, started to blush. She was never without the one thing that kept Raymond's life organized. She was about to speak when Ray finished his request.

"Tonight we do not talk about business, politics, or anything that has to do with our jobs. Tonight we are going to have a great meal, talk about our pasts, and get to know each other better. I have always relied on you to keep things organized, and we have spent a lot of time together, but I don't know much about your history. I know you're a fantastic person, and I enjoy every moment we have together, but I need to know more about my Vice Chancellor. I'm also hoping you want to know more about me. We were thrown together at the worst possible moment in time, almost like two long lost siblings at a funeral. Not the place or time to catch up."

"I agree, Ray. I would also like to know the man I worked for and now work with."

Jocelyn came into the main room of the suite; Raymond had the table set with candles, his clothing had been put away, a fresh pot of coffee was brewing, and in an hour the sun was going to set over the mountains. This was something he wanted share.

"Chef Voutour is preparing a very special dinner for us. I called him this afternoon to place the order."

"You mean the cook that made our lunch last year? The one you asked about his job, and why he does it?"

"Yes, the very one. I made sure he was appointed the head Chef of the Global Community Assembly shortly after our conversation that day."

"Ray, you never cease to surprise me. I have never had the pleasure of working for some on who is so compassionate and really cares about his fellow man."

Ray blushed, thinking this would lead to a conversation about him, but did not want to go that route just yet.

"Thanks, Jocelyn. Would you like a glass of wine? I have some select vintages from all over the world." His tone softened, "I even have some wines from the countries that do not exist anymore. I'm keeping them for special occasions, and to toast the sacrifice its citizens made to preserve their way of life."

Jocelyn looked at the collection. "I'll have the Australian Chardonnay, please."

"Ah, a very good wine indeed. I visited the vineyards a few years ago and I bought a few cases to have shipped home."

"So you collect wine?" Jocelyn took the glass from Ray and sat down in one of the chairs looking out of the picture window. She felt right at home in the blue jeans and new t-shirt the General of the C & C gave her. On the front of the shirt there was a big blue globe with the four continents on it, and a white flag pointing at Salt Lake City. The words "Global Community Command and Control vs. Mother Nature" and on the back a crowd of people on their knees with hands up in the air and the words "Ok, ok...You win, we'll be good!" The C&C thought it was a cute joke in light of what had happened. Raymond approved the t-shirts and requested a few dozen to give out.

"Yes, I've been a wine connoisseur for most of my life. My parents insisted that we all drink one glass of wine a day when I was old enough to drink. We had wine with every super, finally after a couple of years my dad asked me to pick the wine for the evening's meal. I can remember going down to the wine cellar, wine guide book in hand, and spending a good two hours going over the labels and looking them up in the book. Needless to say that night I didn't get the wine in time. Dad came down stairs, grabbed a bottle of his favorite red wine and told me I can either stay here and get tomorrow night's wine, or come up and eat. Well I went up to the supper table, and learned my first lesson. Spending too much time reading about good wine, means you never get to taste it. Dad then said that the subtleties will come in time and to focus on the basics first and never be afraid to experiment. The next night, I had a Chardonnay already chilled and on the table. He was so proud of me."

Raymond sipped from his wine glass, taking a moment to remember his mother and father.

"I guess you could say that is also where I developed a passion to teach. To see the joy on my father's face when he successfully taught something was very contagious; I wanted that feeling too. Hence my goal to be a professor and teach the leaders of tomorrow, little did I know that I was going to be a leader of tomorrow."

Jocelyn raised her glass. "And a damn fine leader at that."

They both laughed, and Jocelyn got up to refresh her glass. Raymond picked up the phone and dialed the kitchen.

"Hi, we're ready, thanks."

"So what is on the menu for tonight?" Jocelyn enquired. "Has Chef Voutour gone out of his way to procure something exotic?"

"I'm not sure...he mentioned roasted lamb, potatoes and vegetables all fresh today, and strawberry shortcake for dessert."

Jocelyn smacked her lips together. "Mmm, my favorite. I haven't had strawberries in years—I can hardly wait."

"You won't have to wait long, I just called."

A knock at the door came as if on cue. Raymond went to open the door as Jocelyn made her way to the table. Ray saw her move and opened the door in a hurried manner, motioned for the kitchen staff to enter and ran over to the table to get the chair for his guest.

"I think it has been longer since someone got my chair for me. Ray, you didn't have to go to all the trouble."

"I wanted to. It's not often I get to say thanks, and I can't say it enough to you."

The kitchen staff served the meal. Ray and Jocelyn cleaned their plates, leaving nothing except the two rib bones on each plate from the lamb. The strawberry shortcake was served in an oversized martini glass: the strawberries were macerated in balsamic vinegar and the whole desert was topped with freshly whipped cream.

As the last spoon rattled in the empty glasses, the kitchen staff had cleaned up and left the suite with Raymond telling them explicitly to thank Chef Voutour from him personally.

"I think we should adjourn to the sitting area, Jocelyn. Would you like some more wine?"

"No thanks Ray, but a cup of coffee would top off a perfect meal."

"OK, coffee it is." Raymond went into the kitchen and grabbed two mugs, he then looked through the counter opening. "Perhaps an Irish Coffee?"

"That sounds wonderful Ray."

Jocelyn looked out the window at the mountains, and the sun was starting to set. The sunsets were brilliant in the Utah area. The deep red of the sun as it shone through the ring was spectacular. The sun would go behind the ring, turn deep red, and just before it set, revert back to a brilliant yellow for a split second.

As Ray brought the coffees over to Jocelyn, she remarked, "Mother Nature sure wanted us to remember that she also has a soft side, didn't she? With sunsets like this every day, it's easy to forget what happened a few months ago."

"You're right. I think she is more beautiful than vengeful; after all, something was seriously wrong and she couldn't breathe, so she fixed the problem. Unfortunately for us we had to go along for the ride."

"You know Ray, I used to marvel at all the wonders on Earth when I was growing up in Florida. My father worked for NASA, he was a safety technician for the Mars colony missions. I can remember him taking the whole family to the Everglades to watch the birds on their migratory flightpath in the fall and in the spring to see them return. Wave after wave would sometimes appear as big dark, flowing masses. Moving with the air currents and appearing fluid weaving around unseen objects. We spent a lot of time on the beach as well, studying the sand dunes, the wildlife and the flora. He wanted us to appreciate everything, and to see how it all fit in one big ecosystem. I wonder if he knew things were as unbalanced as they were?"

Jocelyn took a moment, sipped her coffee, and sighed. "When he passed away, the Mars colony was finally up and running. He was as excited as a little child to have helped put humans on another planet permanently. He embraced any new technology he could: our house was cooled by a geothermal heat pump, electricity produced by solar cells, and we even recharged our own fuel cells.

When I graduated from high school, he had a long talk with me one night on the beach near our house. He told me that I need to know everything I can about the environment and how it interacts with humans. The damage was done in the 20th and 21st centuries, and humans needed to know how to fix it. I don't think he could foresee the environment fixing itself. So I decided to go to University and become and ecological engineer, and my logistical training and organization skills helped me secure a job with your office. I guess after a few years, I made it through the ranks to become your executive assistant and here we are. The rest, they say, is history."

"I remember the day you were hired. I thought you were overqualified for the position, but I'm glad you did not let that stop you. I can honestly say, I don't think there is anyone else in the world who could have done the job any better. Fate brought us together to work as a team and help mankind survive. Cheers to fate."

Raymond and Jocelyn toasted fate, and watched the last light fade from the sky. The stars shone brightly, and a full moon could be seen above the mountains.

Jocelyn took her mug to the sink, rinsed it, and placed it in the dishwasher. She then looked at her watch and went to get her purse. "Thank you for the fantastic evening, Ray. I really have to go and get ready for tomorrow. Interviews in the morning and four viewings in the afternoon will keep me busy."

"Sure. I understand—I have a ton of paperwork to read, and then perhaps on Friday we can work out the next week's schedule to have the Caucus meet and set up their agendas on Monday. We will tour the coast line on Tuesday. I also think we should visit each central Information Center in China, Russia, Brazil and Africa. We'll need to book a jet."

Raymond walked Jocelyn to the door.

"Ok. Thanks again, Raymond. This was the first time in a long time that we didn't have to worry about work. I loved the meal and the company. Good night."

Jocelyn walked down the hall to her suite, and Raymond closed his door. He turned to his tablet, and decided to pour another coffee. The lights came on in his suite and he sat by the picture window. He started to read the daily reports, and began to take notes on what he wanted to accomplish on the upcoming trip.

On the Friday morning, Raymond received a call from the Command and Control Center.

"Dr. Braemore. General Johnstone here."

"Yes, General, how can I help you this morning?

"Sir, your aircraft is fueled and ready for departure at 10:00 hours. I've sent you a copy of the flight plan and I would advise being on the tarmac about thirty minutes before departure."

"Ok. Thanks General, I'll be there."

Raymond and Jocelyn met on the elevator again, with their baggage in tow.

"This is going to be a very interesting flight, I think. No one but the Red Cross Emergency Response teams has seen the coastlines since the disaster."

"I know. I'm a little excited, and somewhat nervous. If we didn't know that there were cities and towns there before, it would just be a sightseeing flight, but a lot of people died and a lot of property was lost. This will be our first survey of the disaster areas."

Raymond nodded in agreement as they left the C&C to the tarmac. They walked up to a sleek shiny silver jet with GCN painted on the tail. The Lockheed SS853 was the latest iteration of the supersonic, sub orbital jets produced in the last twenty years. This aircraft was capable of flying at fifteen miles, at a speed of mach 5. The occupant quarters were pressurized and luxurious, having the capability of circumnavigating the globe three times on a single charge of the fuel cells and magnetic engines.

Raymond and Jocelyn entered the cabin; Stuart was there and greeted both with an eager wave.

"Welcome aboard, Ray and Jocelyn. I hope you

don't mind, but when I heard that this flight was going to take place, I just had to see things for myself."

"Not at all Stuart. I'm glad you came along to describe some of the things we'll be looking at." Raymond reached out to shake Stuart's hand. Stuart then shook Jocelyn's hand, and whispered, "Congratulations, Vice Chancellor." Everyone made their way to the seats and stowed their gear: each seat was next to a window and a working table. The tables were equipped with satellite phones, internet hookup, and an extra video screen. Once the last seatbelt was clipped the aircraft started to taxi.

They were airborne in three minutes, and the aircraft rose through a steady climb to five miles and headed north east. The trip would take them down the eastern coast of North America, over the equatorial ocean and along the eastern coast of Brazil, where a stop at the Capital Information Center would be for a 1:00 p.m. meeting. After an hour, they would continue south, and rise to 10 miles in altitude to travel west along Antarctica's northern coast, and then head north over the Australian Islands, and North East to fly over the Hawaiian Islands. They will then turn west and visit the China, Russian and African Capital Information

Centers. The aircraft is scheduled to return to base after 36 hours.

Stuart marveled at the complete reshaping of the coast lines of all the continents. From his vantage point, everything was washed away, or buried in tons of sediment. The oceans cleaned the coast lines of anything mankind had put there, established new salt marshes, and wildlife was thriving. It was critical that these areas be protected until they could get reestablished and the Global Community Assembly outlawed any coastal development for five years. There was a 50 mile buffer zone, and recreational visits were strictly enforced. Most citizens did not have a problem with these rules; they were too busy to have any recreational time this early into the rebuilding process.

Raymond's report to the Global Community Information Channel detailed the progress each area had made and the challenges they still faced. Raymond made sure the needs and requirements were passed to the right departments, and skilled engineers and technicians who were available to travel and help were recruited from the Information Center's database. These people would receive a page or text message, and could choose if they wanted to go.

FORCED EVOLUTION

After his reporting duties were finished he reflected on the past year. He was pleased with the way things were working out. He thought of how nearly every human being in the world had to put aside their differences, their preconceptions, and started fresh. Everyone was the same inside, yet different outside. It was these differences that made mankind unique. The vast cultures, languages and beliefs were secondary to the simple fact that we were all human and had to survive. He read reports of great sacrifices and heroic deeds, of opposing political factions coming together to help one another. Raymond became philosophical for a moment, thinking how strange it was—if you let a man, a community, a country think too long, they will find a way to hate, conquer, or destroy something they cannot have. But if you take away their need to have those thoughts and present them with the raw pure instinctive need to survive, those thoughts do not return. He suspected that the brain resets itself if it has to run on pure instinct for a long time. Mankind has gone through many changes, and as a species, this forced evolution will ensure that the next chapter in its history is one of peace and growth.

Raymond wrote these thoughts down. He was

sure someday soon he would have to repeat them to a very large crowd. He got up from his chair and undressed on his way to bed. He did not hang anything up, or take out anything for the morning. He was exhausted and just wanted to sleep. He was snoring before the head hit the pillow.

Chapter 10

Mr. and Mrs. Bowing woke to a bright sunny morning. The roosters were celebrating another successful night, and the cows walked out of the barn to the fields. Steve was the first out of bed and made his way down to the kitchen. He walked around gathering the items for breakfast and to make coffee: this morning it was cold cereal with fresh milk and strawberries. Steve moved with fluid motion to get things ready; he was going to try and serve his new bride breakfast in bed. He quickly poured a cup of coffee, added a splash of milk, cut the strawberries, put them on the cereal, and added some sugar and milk. He looked at the tray—something was missing. A flower, he thought. He went to the back porch with a pair of scissors to cut the first fresh flower he could find.

Jocelyn heard the back door close as she made her way down to the kitchen. A smile came across her face when she saw what Steve was planning. She quickly turned around and ran upstairs to the bedroom. She started to laugh when she heard Steve outside, trying to find the perfect flower and mumbling to himself. She quickly took her robe off and messed up the freshly-made bed. Then just as she was pulling the covers up to her neck Steve came through the door with a tray and one sorry looking daisy.

"Good morning, Mrs. Bowing. I thought you might like to start the day off with breakfast in bed." He looked his wife's red face: and she was shaking with stifled laughter. Tears started to form at the corners of her eyes.

"Oh god, that is perfect, Steve. And I have to confess, I knew about your surprise a few minutes ago."

"I knew that, I saw you running up the stairs, which is why I grabbed the first flower I could find. I have to have some element of surprise." As he said that a couple of petals fell off of the daisy, and Steve almost dropped the tray.

"I'll go finish cleaning up and then start the morning chores, honey."

"Ok. Thank you for the lovely breakfast. I love you."

"I love you too." Steve returned to the kitchen. This morning he was just going to have coffee: he poured a cup and made his way out to the barn.

There were some unusual noises coming from the pig pens. Steve grabbed the feed bucket and walked over to see the two big sows nursing another fifteen piglets.

"Well, I see it has been an eventful evening at the old sow home. Good news for you two," and looking at the other pigs in the corner, "bad news for some of you." He put the feed into the hopper and turned on the water system. As the pigs came to feed, he looked for the five biggest sows and decided to mark them for removal. He made a mental note to talk to Barry today and see when would be a good time to have them picked up. The five he selected would not be going outside today and most likely never again. He would separate them into another pen in the other barn, and keep them there until pickup. Since it was a Saturday, perhaps tomorrow Barry's son could come and get them.

Steve went to the chicken coop and harvested the eggs, fed the chickens and changed the water. He noticed that his pen was rather cramped and decided to expand it next week. He would have to segregate some of the hens and roosters so they could breed, but it would only mean a dozen less eggs. He thought that one hundred chickens would be a good number and easy to manage.

The cows were low maintenance: fresh hay in the barn and water in the trough and his morning chores were done. He put his tools away, started the composter and made his way back to the kitchen for another cup of coffee and perhaps a bowl of cereal.

That evening, Steve and Jenna made their way over to Barry's farm. He called around noon and said that the wedding reception was at his place, and to be there promptly at six. They drove through down the 12A to Interstate 89, headed west and then on to the North Hartland Road for Barry's farm. They found the entrance well marked and a long winding driveway brought them up to the main house, which was the former clubhouse.

"It was nice for Barry to throw a reception for us."

Steve nodded, "Yes, I'll have to tell him how much we appreciate it. From the looks of things I think this is going to be big."

Steve maneuvered the truck to the parking lot, and right up front was a spot reserved for Mr. and Mrs. Bowing. Barry was there, sitting on a golf cart, waiting to escort the guests of honor to the big ball room. Jenna and Steve just sat in the truck for a moment to take it all in. Barry was becoming impatient.

"Come on, you two. Your chariot awaits, and your driver needs a drink." A big smile on Barry's face made Steve and Jenna jump out of their truck and on to the cart.

Steve put his arm around Jenna and raising one arm, "Driver, once around the block, through the park and on to the festivities."

Barry made a whipping motion, "Heya, giddy up!" and put his foot down on the accelerator. The golf cart jumped and headed towards what was once the 18th green, now a converted patio visible from the back of the clubhouse. The sand traps had been converted to sand boxes for Barry's kids and the huge deck overlooking the green fully decorated with green balloons, and torches were placed around the entire area. Music was playing from the sound system and the band was getting warmed up. Jenna could not believe her eyes.

"Steve, can you believe this? It's so beautiful."

"Yes, Barry did a fantastic job."

Barry stopped the cart in the middle of the green, and whistled for everyone to pay attention to him. He whistled a few more times before the only sound you could hear was the crickets.

"Ladies and Gentlemen...welcome! I present to you Mr. and Mrs. Bowing."

Steve and Jenna waved to the crowd of over 300 people and made their way up to the patio where a line was forming for formal greetings. Most of the people at the reception were patrons of the markets and people they met when they attended the weekly social gatherings. The people in the line congratulated Steve and Jenna, making references to the great job they did when they took over the Steve's farm. Many offered accolades and assistance in working the land and running the market. The Bowings were very grateful and thanked every person they met. After the procession was complete, Steve was called upon to make a speech on behalf of the happy couple. Not being much of a public speaker, but filled with pride in his new home town, Steve took the microphone and stood on the stage.

"Jenn and I would like to thank everyone who came out tonight. We are overwhelmed by your kindness. We came to White River Junction with the hopes of setting up shop to take care of the residents. We did not expect to be running a farm, but I guess you should take the cards you're dealt and play the hand. I cannot say enough about

Richard and Maryann Steve. Their foresight and thoughtfulness enabled Jenna and I to get the farm running as if we had been doing this all our lives. I have come to know Richard Steve through his teaching videos and can truly appreciate his expertise and patience. Maryann's home was left in perfect condition and we are very grateful for everything they did for us. I would like to take a moment to toast Richard and Maryann Steve."

Everyone applauded and toasted the former residents who made the ultimate sacrifice for the love of their family. A few minutes of good words and Steve continued. "I met Jenna back in New York City when we were being evacuated. Over the course of the trip, we talked and speculated about what was going to happen. We decided to stick next to each other no matter what and helped in any way we could. Jenna and I spent the darkest days supporting each other and talking about what we would like to do afterwards. When we were permitted to head out, I immediately thought of White River Junction. We decided to venture out and see what we could do to start over. When we found the Steves' farm, we couldn't believe our luck, and fell in love with the place. Our plans changed, and the rest, as they say, is history."

Steve looked at Jenna, smiled and took a sip from his champagne glass.

"Now, as you know, we have been working hard to start growing produce on the farm and raise the animals. Our market shelves are starting to show progress and I'm sure over the next couple of weeks we'll be up to full production. I know that I could have never done this much is such a short time without my best friend's support and encouragement. Her hard work has made mine easier, and for that sweetheart, I thank you.

I know no one can tell us what the future will hold as we become comfortable in our new roles, but so long as Jenna is by my side, I'm sure we'll manage and grow as a family. The Bowing farm is always open to you and your families to visit any time.

I want to thank Barry for arranging this celebration and you all for coming. Have fun. Now, if someone would tell the band to start playing, I would like to have a dance with my wife."

Steve put the microphone down and kissed Jenna. The band started to play a waltz and for the first time since they met, Steve and Jenna danced.

The celebrations went on into the wee hours of the morning. Steve and Jenna spent most of the time on the dance floor. Jenna was swept away by the man she loved. She did not let go, wanting to spend every minute dancing on the patio under a brilliant full moon and flickering torches.

When they had said their final goodbyes and thank yous, Jenna and Steve walked to their truck, arm in arm like two teenagers under the spell of summer love. Steve opened the door for Jenna and she thanked him; he walked around the front and got in. As they pulled away, the music could still be heard and the lights of the patio were moving with the motion of the people still dancing.

"That was fantastic, Steve. I'll never forget this night."

"I'm glad; it was a reception to remember.

Oh, Barry will be sending one of his boys over tomorrow to pick up the pigs. Don't worry, I told him to make it late afternoon."

Steve smiled and winked at Jenna. As the truck turned onto the highway and headed home, Jenna slid across her seat and cuddled against him.

"I think I can finally say I'm going home."

Printed in the United States
134028LV00002B/103-150/P